Witch Is Why The Owl Returned

Published by Implode Publishing Ltd
© Implode Publishing Ltd 2017

The right of Adele Abbott to be identified as the Author of the Work has been asserted by her in accordance with the Copyright, Designs and Patents Act 1988.

All rights reserved, worldwide.
No part of this publication may be reproduced, stored in a retrieval system, or transmitted, in any form or by any means without the prior written permission of the copyright owner.

The characters and events in this book are fictitious. Any similarity to real persons, dead or alive, is purely coincidental and not intended by the author.

Chapter 1

"Is the mirror broken?" I said.

"Which mirror?" Jack looked up from his bowl of muesli.

"Your shaving-mirror."

"No. Why?"

"I assumed you must have been shaving blind, judging by the number of cuts on your face."

"I'm still half asleep. I didn't get home until about one."

"I didn't hear you come in."

"I know. You never stopped snoring."

"I do not snore. I have never snored."

"Sorry, my mistake. We must have an injured animal hiding in the bedroom. Maybe I should check the wardrobes?"

"I do not snore. What were you working on that kept you out so late?"

"Nothing, as it turned out. There was a report of a body in the canal. Half of the station was down there, but it turned out to be a shop mannequin floating on the water."

"How could anyone not know the difference between a body and a mannequin?"

"That's what I'd like to know. Although, in fairness, it is pitch black on that stretch of the canal. All of the street lights have been out for months now. What about you? Are you up to anything exciting at the moment?"

"Not really. Unless you consider going over my year-end accounts with Luther exciting."

"Have you had a good year?"

"Define *'good'*."

"Did you end up in profit?"

"Don't you remember I told you that profits are so *passé*?"

"You did tell me that, but I'm not sure I believe it. Did you at least do better than last year?"

"Of course. Much better."

"Are you working on any cases at the moment?"

"Not really, but that's how it's always been: peaks and troughs. There's no telling who or what might come through my door today. Anyway, why are we talking about work? I thought we'd made a pact to keep work out of the home?"

"You're right, sorry. I just wanted to say that I'm really chuffed that you and Mum hit it off the second time around."

"Me too. I like Yvonne."

"When I look at Mum and Dad, it makes me realise that I want the same kind of relationship for us. They've been together for so long, and yet they're as close now as they've always been. And do you know what the secret to their success is?"

"Matching jumpers?"

"It's honesty. They've never had any secrets. Mum knows everything about Dad, and vice versa."

Oh yeah. Apart from the whole witchfinder thing. "You can't possibly know that."

"Of course I do. They tell each other everything—absolutely everything. They never keep secrets from one another."

"Look, I get that you think the world of your parents, and so do I. They're both great, but how can you possibly know that your father doesn't have some deep, dark secret that he's never told your mother? She'd never know and neither would you."

"You can't live with someone for that long, and still keep a secret from them. It's impossible. You saw how they are together at the anniversary party." He grinned. "Speaking of which, it's our anniversary soon."

"What anniversary?"

"It's two years since we first met."

"Is it? Are you sure? It feels like much longer."

"I'm positive. I have a note in my diary."

"What diary? You don't keep a diary."

"I've always kept one."

"You're making it up. Show me."

He walked out into the hallway, and returned with a small black book. "Here it is."

"That just goes to prove my point."

"What point?"

"That it's possible to keep secrets from someone you live with."

"My diary isn't a secret."

"How come I've never seen it, then?"

"I always keep it in my jacket pocket."

"And when do you write in it?"

"I don't do it every day. Only when there's something noteworthy."

"Oh? Meeting me was noteworthy, was it?"

"Of course it was."

"Ah, that's sweet." I gave him a peck on the lips. "Hold on. If it was two years ago, how come you still have that same diary?"

"It's a five-year one."

"Let me have a look."

"No. It's private."

"I thought you just said that you had no secrets."

"But this is my diary. That's different."

"No, it isn't. You either believe in *no secrets* or you don't. Which is it to be?"

"Alright, but when you read the entry, just keep in mind that I'd only just met you."

"Okay. Let me see."

"I wouldn't want you to read too much into what I wrote back then."

"Just give it here." I snatched it from his hand, and flicked back to a date two years earlier. There was room for five days' entries on each page, which explained why the diary was so thin. All the entries were blank, so I flicked forward a few pages.

"*Met Jill Gooder — a P.I. A real smartass. She is going to be trouble*?" I glared at him.

"I warned you."

I couldn't keep up the straight face. "It's okay. I don't keep a diary, but if I did, I'm pretty sure I would have said much worse about you."

"Are you telling me it wasn't love at first sight for you?" He grinned. "I'm hurt."

"You do realise what this diary means, don't you?"

"What?"

"You owe me a secret."

"What are you talking about?"

"You've kept a secret diary ever since we've been together. That means you owe me a secret."

"Do you have any?"

"No, but if I did, you couldn't complain about it because it would just make us even."

"Can I have my diary back?"

"Perhaps I should take a look through it to check if there are any other women mentioned in here?"

"Give it here." He snatched it back.

"What are we going to do to celebrate our anniversary?" I said.

"I thought we might have a night out somewhere."

"As long as you're paying."

"Don't I always?"

***

Not long after Jack had left for work, Kathy phoned.

"I need your advice, Jill."

"Very funny. Why did you really call?"

"It's true. I really would appreciate your advice. I've been offered a new job."

"Where?"

"It's a new shop which is going to open just up the road from Ever. Do you remember that shop where they served the weird drinks through those enormous straws?"

"The Final Straw?"

"Yeah, that was it. A company called YarnStormers has bought their old place."

"You've been headhunted?"

"It looks like it. From what they've told me so far, it sounds as though they have big plans."

"I take it from the name that they'll be competition for Ever?"

"Yeah. Your grandmother will be livid when she finds out that they're opening."

"Doesn't she know yet?"

"She can't do or I'd have heard about it."

"She'll go ballistic if you decide to take the job."

"Do you think I should?"

"I don't know why you're asking me."

"I value your opinion."

"Since when?"

"Come on, Jill."

"What does Peter think?"

"He says I should go for it."

"Why don't we consider the pros and cons? First the pros: I assume it will be more money?"

"Quite a bit more."

"If you're the manager, you'll be the one doling out the orders instead of taking them from Grandma."

"That would be nice. I wouldn't have to worry about covering a tea room and roof terrace either. I'd just have the shop to look after."

"And then of course, there's the biggest plus of all."

"Which is?"

"No Grandma."

"That's a really big plus." She laughed. "But there are some cons as well."

"Such as?"

"I'd have to work longer hours, so I'd have to find a way to make that work with the kids."

"Will you be able to do that?"

"I should be able to sort something out. Also, there'll be more pressure because I'll be the one responsible for everything."

"You can handle that, can't you?"

"I think so. At least I would be the one making the decisions. But the thing that worries me most is what kind of reaction I'll get from your grandmother. She's only just given me a pay rise."

"I'd forgotten about that. Still, this is your life. You have to make the right decision for you and your family. If Grandma doesn't like it, she'll just have to lump it."

"That's easy for you to say. You aren't the one who has to tell her that you're leaving."

"Does that mean you've decided to take the job?"

"Not one-hundred per cent. I don't have to let YarnStormers know straight away. Pete and I will need to give it more thought before I make a final decision."

"Let me know what you decide. If you are going to take it, I want to make sure I'm not around when Grandma finds out. Now, while I've got you, I wanted to ask if Lizzie had said anything about our visit to Washbridge House? I got the impression she didn't really enjoy herself."

"She was a bit disappointed, that's all. She reckons there wasn't a single ghost there. To be honest, I was hoping she might have got over this crazy obsession with ghosts by now, but there's no sign of it ending."

"I wouldn't worry about it. She's bound to grow out of it soon enough. Oh well, I suppose I'd better be making tracks. Good luck with your job deliberations."

Mad and I had taken Lizzie to Washbridge House because it was supposedly haunted. Except that it wasn't. If there had been any ghosts, we would have seen them. Mad had always been able to see ghosts, and since I'd learned how to travel to Ghost Town, I also had the ability to see them at will. None of us had seen any. After we'd dropped a disappointed Lizzie back home, Mad and I discussed the possible reasons for the total absence of ghosts. We came to the conclusion that the rumour about the house being haunted must have been started by the owners to attract more visitors.

***

When I pulled up at the toll booth, Mr Ivers was dressed in a smart suit, and was acting rather strangely. And when I say *strangely*, I mean even by his standards. Instead of sitting next to the kiosk window, he was standing side on, with his hand stretched out towards me. I couldn't drop the cash into his hand because for some unfathomable reason, he had his palm face-down.

"Mr Ivers!"

"Jill? I didn't notice you there."

That was clearly a lie because we had made eye-contact as I'd driven towards the booth.

"You're looking very debonair today, Mr Ivers."

"This?" He brushed the lapel with his hand. "This is just some old suit I threw on."

It clearly wasn't. It was quite obviously new, and looked very expensive.

"Mr Ivers." I had to prompt him because his hand was still palm-down. "Don't you want the toll fee?"

"You're probably wondering about the watch." He pushed his hand closer to my face, and for the first time I noticed his timepiece.

"That looks expensive."

"It was, but worth every penny, wouldn't you say?"

I'd seen Jack drooling over watches like that one, and they didn't come cheap. It must have cost somewhere in the region of two thousand pounds.

"It's very nice. Did you come into some money?"

"In a manner of speaking. My new newsletter, Toppers News, is selling like hot cakes. Norman, at Top Of The World, can barely keep pace with demand."

"Congratulations." Who would have thought there were so many toppers (nutters) out there?

"I've been invited to ToppersCon next week, to sign copies of the newsletter for my fans."

"Is that some kind of convention?"

"The biggest in the country for Toppers. There'll be thousands there. I have a spare ticket, if you'd care to accompany me."

"I'd love to, but I'm so busy at the moment that I won't be able to make it. You should try and catch Jack—I'm sure he'd love to go."

"Do you think so?"

"Oh yeah. He absolutely loves bottle tops."

"Great. I'll keep a look out for him."

That was my anniversary present to Jack sorted then.

Snigger.

Chapter 2

It was Jules' day off, so Mrs V was by herself in the office. For once, she wasn't knitting; instead she had lots of papers spread out over both desks.

"Morning, Jill. Lovely morning."

"It's cold and raining."

"But apart from that—quite lovely."

"You look busy, Mrs V."

"I am, dear. I've found myself a new hobby."

"Instead of knitting?"

"Don't be silly. Nothing could ever replace my affection for yarn, but I do now have something else to occupy myself while I'm here."

"As well as your work, you mean?"

"What work?"

"Good point. What is it you're up to?"

"I'm tracing my family tree. Armi got me into it. He's managed to trace his own family back through five generations."

"Did he find any skeletons in the cupboard?"

"Not really. It would appear that his family have always been involved with the law. Most of them were solicitors of one kind or another."

"Have you managed to make much progress with your own family tree?"

"Not so far, but then I did only start a few days ago. Have you ever thought of tracing your ancestry, Jill?"

"No. It doesn't really interest me."

"You really should. You might find something surprising."

More surprising than having a witch for a mother, and a

wizard for a father? Somehow, I doubted it.

When I walked into my office, Winky was on the sofa; he seemed engrossed in something on his phone. His little paws were tapping the screen so fast, it was a wonder he didn't break it.

"Morning, Winky."

"Shush! I'm busy."

Charming. "What are you up to?"

"Can't talk now. I'm at a critical stage."

"Of what?"

"B.U.S.Y."

"Okay, okay. Keep your fur on."

After the con trick he'd played on me with the Salmon Emporium, I should have known better than to pay him any attention. That still didn't stop me wanting to know what he was up to.

I'd barely had chance to sort through my pencils before Mrs V came through to my office.

"Jill, I'm ever so sorry, but last Friday, I forgot to mention that a Mrs Brownling called. I booked her in for an appointment with you this morning, but then forgot to add it to the diary."

"Never mind. It's not like I'm run off my feet. What time is she due?"

"She's actually here now."

"Okay. You'd better send her in."

Mrs V glanced at Winky. "I really don't know why you let that stupid cat have your phone. He'll break it."

"You're right." I walked over to the sofa, and snatched it from him.

Before he could complain, Mrs V had shown Mrs

Brownling in. She was a tall woman with greying hair, and a nice line in fingerless gloves.

"Would you like a drink, Mrs Brownling?" Mrs V asked.

"Not for me, thanks." She turned to me. "Thank you for seeing me, Ms Gooder. You must be extremely busy."

"Oh, yes. Very. Won't you take a seat?"

"Thank you." She removed her coat and fingerless gloves. "Do you do much work in connection with missing people, Ms Gooder?"

"Please call me Jill."

"Okay, and you must call me Sophie."

"I've worked on a few missing person cases. Is that why you're here today?"

"Yes, it's my daughter, Angie Potts."

"When did she go missing?"

"Twenty years ago, tomorrow."

I hadn't seen that one coming. "Twenty years?"

"It feels like a hundred."

"It must do. I have to ask, why come to me now? After all this time?"

"You're my last hope. The police gave up looking a long time ago."

"Are you sure about that? They rarely close the case on a missing person until—" I caught myself just in time.

"Until they find a body? It's okay. I realise that's probably the best outcome I can expect, but at least that would give me some kind of closure. As for the police, they say that the case is still on-going, but they're not doing anything to find Angie. Don't get me wrong. I understand that they have limited resources, and it makes sense to utilise those on cases which might still have a positive outcome, but that doesn't help me."

"I have to be honest with you, Sophie. After such a long time, the chances of me finding anything are remote."

"I understand that, and I won't hold it against you if you don't come up with anything, but some hope is better than none. Do you think you'll be able to fit it around your existing workload?"

"It won't be easy, but I'm sure I'll manage."

"Thank you so much. You don't know how much this means to me."

"I take it your daughter is married?"

"No. Why?"

"She doesn't have the same surname as you."

"Oh, right. No. that's because I remarried, but Angie kept her birth name."

"I see. Can you talk me through what happened on the day your daughter disappeared?"

"I still remember it as though it was yesterday. Angie had just turned twenty. She was a quiet girl, and was still living at home with me and her stepfather, Lionel. Her real dad died when she was thirteen. Lionel and I got together when Angie was fifteen."

"Did they get along okay?"

"For the most part, but they were never what you would call close. On the night she disappeared, Angie had been on a night out with three of her girlfriends. The others made it home okay, but Angie never came back."

"A night out? Where had they been?"

"It was one of her friends' twentieth birthday. They went out for a meal, and then for drinks around the town centre. At the end of the night, they went their separate ways."

"Why didn't they travel home together?"

"They lived in different areas in and around Washbridge."

"When did you realise something was wrong?"

"When it got to three o' clock in the morning. I never slept when Angie was out late; I couldn't settle until I heard her come in. She was never later than two o'clock, and that was only if they went on to a nightclub."

"Had they been to a club that night?"

"No. It was a weekday, so they called it a night just after eleven, but I wasn't aware of that. At three o' clock, I woke Lionel; he went to look for her while I called the police. That's when the nightmare began." Sophie put her bag on my desk, and took out a box file. "There's every press cutting since the time she disappeared in here. It might be best if I left this with you, so you can go through it."

"Thanks. That will be very helpful."

"If you have any questions, just get in touch. My number and email address are on the side of the box."

As soon as Sophie Brownling had walked out of my office, Winky jumped onto my desk.

"Phone!" he demanded.

"What's the magic word?"

"Now!"

"What were you doing on there, anyway? You seemed to be very engrossed."

"Are you going to give it to me, or do I have to report you to the Cats Protection League?"

"And say what? That I wouldn't let you have your phone? That, I have to see."

He obviously had no intention of telling me what he was up to, so I let him have his phone back.

Just then, my phone rang; it was Aunt Lucy.

"Jill, are you busy?"

"Not particularly."

"I'm shopping in Candlefield at the moment. Could we meet in Cuppy C?"

"Sure. I'm feeling a little peckish anyway. I'll meet you, there."

"Peckish?" Winky laughed.

"And what's so funny about that?"

"You're always eating. I reckon you must have worms."

"I do not have worms; I just have a healthy appetite. And besides, everything I eat is perfectly healthy."

"Really? So, what will you be having to eat at Cuppy C?"

"Not that it's any of your business, but I'll more than likely have blueberries."

"And these blueberries? What form will they take?"

"I don't have time for idle chit-chat with you. Why don't you make yourself useful, and clean up some of the cat hairs in here?"

I magicked myself over to Cuppy C.

"Stupid cats!"

"Sorry?" Amber looked confused.

"Nothing, it's just that cat of mine. He's driving me insane."

"Right. What can I get for you?"

"Do you have any blueberries?"

"Only those inside the muffins."

"I suppose they will have to do."

What? I tried, didn't I?

"Have you told Jill our big news?" Pearl had come through from the cake shop.

"It would be big news if you two didn't have big news for once. What is it this time?"

"We're going to host a book signing here on Friday."

"That's certainly different. Who's the author?"

"Tammy Winestock."

"Not *the* Tammy Winestock? Never heard of her."

"*Never heard of Tammy Winestock*?" Amber said. "Are you being serious?"

"Deadly. Should I have?"

"She's famous." Pearl produced a book from under the counter. "Look!"

The title of the book was '101 Winning Recipes'.

"It's been in the bestseller charts for over a year," Amber said. "And she's just published her follow-up book: 'Another 101 Winning Recipes'."

"Imaginative name."

"This place is going to be packed." Pearl looked very pleased with herself. "I'm not sure how we're going to accommodate everyone."

"Maybe you could get Tammy to sit next to the drive-thru serving hatch, and have people queue in the alleyway to get their books signed."

If looks could kill, I would have been stone dead.

"We don't talk about the serving hatch," Pearl snapped.

"Sorry. Just my little joke."

Fortunately, Aunt Lucy arrived before the twins had a chance to tear me limb from limb.

"Sorry I'm late, Jill. I met Jessica Hillslope. That woman could talk the hind legs off an ostrich."

Huh?

"That's okay. The twins were just telling me about the book signing they've organised."

"I haven't heard anything about that."

"That's because you never come in here, Mum," Pearl said.

"Of course I do—whenever I'm passing. So, who's the author?"

"Ta-da!" Pearl brought out the book again.

"Tammy Winestock?" Aunt Lucy was clearly impressed. "How did you manage to sign her up?"

"Nothing to it," Amber said. "Her agent contacted us, and asked if we'd be interested."

"But this place is so small?" Aunt Lucy glanced around the shop. "Will there be enough room?"

I considered mentioning my suggestion about the serving hatch, but thought better of it. I couldn't afford to upset the twins again—at least not until I had my muffin and latte.

"Will you come, Mum?" Pearl said.

"Definitely." Aunt Lucy sounded genuinely enthusiastic. "I'm a big fan."

Once Aunt Lucy and I had our cakes and drinks, I led the way to the table that was furthest away from the counter.

"I take it that this Tammy Winestock is a big deal?" I said.

"She's probably the most famous celebrity chef in Candlefield. She's always on the TV. I'm just amazed that she'd want to make a personal appearance in Cuppy C. Credit where credit is due; it's quite a coup for the twins."

Hmm. My 'something smells fishy-ometer' was beginning to beep.

"You said you wanted to talk to me about something, Aunt Lucy?"

"Yes. My neighbour, Biddy Tranter, is moving out. Her husband has got himself a job in the human world; they're moving to Washbridge. Biddy is an avid knitter, and is hoping to find a knitting group once she's settled into her new home. I told her about Mrs V, and I promised I'd ask if you'd have a word to see if she might be able to give Biddy any advice."

"No problem. I'm sure Mrs V will put her right."

"Thanks, Jill. To tell you the truth, I'll be really sorry to see Biddy and Brian leave. I just hope I don't get landed with bad neighbours."

"I shouldn't worry. I'm sure it will be fine."

"How are things with you? I hear that Jack's mother came to visit."

"She did, and I'm pleased to report that we got on like a house on fire."

"That's good to hear. I know you were a little worried about her after the anniversary party."

"That was my bad. I let my imagination get the better of me, and saw things that weren't there."

"I'm glad you've cleared the air."

"Definitely. I feel like I know her much better now."

The darling little witchfinder.

Chapter 3

I was dreading going back to the office because I had a meeting arranged with Luther. Normally, that would have been one of the highlights of my day, but he was coming in to go over my year-end accounts. That was never fun.

Before that, I had thirty minutes to kill, so I called in at Ever. It was unusually quiet; Kathy was daydreaming behind the counter.

"Does Chloe know you've been offered another job?"

"No. I haven't said anything, and I probably won't unless I decide to take it."

"You still haven't made your mind up then?"

"No. One minute, I think I'd be crazy not to take it, and then the next, I think I'd be insane to leave this job. I almost wish they'd never approached me. Are you here to see your grandmother?"

"No. I'm just killing a few minutes before my meeting with Luther."

"Why the long face? I thought you liked him?"

"I do, but we're going to be discussing my year-end accounts."

"That sounds exciting."

"Terrifying, more like. Peter will have to do those too, now that he's his own boss. Has he found himself an accountant yet?"

"I'm not sure. I haven't heard him mention one."

"You should tell him to contact Luther."

"Are you on commission?"

"I wish."

Just then, a loud banging noise came from under our

feet.

"What's that?" I said.

"I've no idea. They've been at it all day. They must have just come back from their break."

"Who?"

"There are five or six workmen down there. They turned up first thing this morning, and asked for your grandmother. The next thing I knew, they were on their way down to the basement."

"To do what?"

"How would I know? I only work here. I did ask, but your grandmother ignored my question. I even asked one of the workmen, but he said that the old woman had threatened to do unspeakable things to them if they discussed the work with anyone. No doubt we'll find out in due course."

"No doubt. Oh, well, I suppose I'd better get this over with. Wish me luck."

***

When I arrived at the office, Luther was looking at Mrs V's family tree.

"That's really fascinating, Mrs V." He almost sounded as though he meant it. "Are you ready to make a start, Jill?"

"As ready as I'll ever be."

I led the way through to my office.

"Did you realise that the cat has your phone?" Luther gestured to Winky who was on the sofa.

"Ah! So that's where I left it." I just managed to avoid Winky's claws, as I took it from him.

"So? How are the accounts looking, Luther? Much better than last year, I bet?"

"There's a definite improvement."

"That's good."

"But then, last year's figures were terrible. This year's figures are just bad."

"Are you sure? Could you have miscalculated?"

"I'm an accountant, Jill. I don't miscalculate."

"No, of course not. Is there anything I need to give particular attention to?"

"Yes. First, you are still using your business credit card to pay for things that quite obviously are not business expenses."

"That's not me. That's—" I glanced at Winky.

"Sorry? How do you mean it wasn't you?"

"I—err—I meant I don't know why I did that. It won't happen again."

"Good. The other major problem is cash."

"What about it?"

"You aren't making enough of it. Your caseload fluctuates so much that there are periods when you are overloaded, and other times when you have no work at all."

"I'm not sure what I can do about that."

"What you really need is a source of regular income."

"Isn't that called a 'job'?"

"Not necessarily. There must be certain businesses who have a need for regular P.I. services. Debt collectors? That sort of thing."

"Work for a firm of debt collectors? Don't you think enough people hate me already?"

"It doesn't have to be debt collectors. There must be

other companies who could contract your services on a regular basis. If you could find something that would keep you going through the lean months, your accounts would be in much better shape."

"Okay. I'll give it some thought."

"Good. And don't forget that the four of us are supposed to be having another night out some time."

"I haven't forgotten, but Jack has been very busy. He didn't get in until the early hours of this morning."

"A big case?"

"Yeah. Mannequin homicide."

"Sorry?"

"I'm just joking. Anyway, how are things with you and Maria?"

"Couldn't be better. She's on the lookout for a job."

"Doing what?"

"Her experience is in retail, but I think she'll consider anything. If you hear of any vacancies, let me know, would you?"

"Will do."

"Do you mind?" As soon as Luther was out of the door, Winky snatched back his phone.

"You should keep it out of sight when I have visitors. I could hardly tell Luther that it belonged to you, could I?"

"How am I meant to get my new business venture off the ground if I can't access my phone?"

"What business venture would that be?"

Why was I asking? When would I ever learn?

"I don't suppose you'll let up until I tell you." He sighed. "If you must know, I'm putting my app through its final testing."

"You've downloaded an app? What's so exciting about that?"

"I haven't *downloaded* an app. I've created it. Once I've finished the final testing, it will be launched onto the market."

"You? Create an app? I don't believe you. You don't have the necessary skillset."

"I didn't create it myself. I hired someone on Hire-A-Moggy. His rates were very reasonable."

"What does it do, this app of yours? Can I see it?" I reached for his phone.

"No." He pulled away. "This is top secret. I don't want you copying my idea."

***

Megan was just about to go into her house when I pulled up on my driveway.

"Megan! Do you have a minute?"

"Sure. Would you like to come in for a drink?"

"No, thanks. It's my turn to make dinner. I just wanted to ask you something."

"Okay."

"My receptionist's sister is hoping to get into the modelling business, but she doesn't have a clue where to start. I said I'd ask you if you had any advice to offer her."

"The best advice I can give her is not to do it. It's a cut-throat business with some horrible people in it."

"I'm sure you're right, but I doubt that's what she wants to hear."

"What's her name?"

"Lules."

"That's an unusual name."

"It's actually Lulu, but everyone calls her Lules."

"What does she do at the moment?"

"She's working in a black pudding factory."

"Oh?"

"Apparently, she was Miss Black Pudding 2017."

"Right." Megan smiled. "Why don't you give her my number? I'll have a chat with her. If I can't talk her out of it, I can at least give her a few contact numbers, and warn her about the pitfalls to watch out for."

"That's very kind. Are you sure you don't mind?"

"Not at all. If I can save someone from the misery I went through when I first started out in the business, it will be well worth it."

"Thanks. I take it that things with you and Ryan are okay now?"

"Yeah. I suppose."

"You don't sound very sure. What's wrong?"

"It's probably just me. It feels like I'm always finding fault with him."

"Something is obviously bothering you."

"While I was at his place last weekend, I was thirsty, so I checked the fridge for juice." Her voice trailed away.

"And?"

"It was full of bottles with some strange, dark red liquid in them."

Oh bum! What was wrong with that guy? Did he have no sense at all?

"What kind of dark red liquid?"

"That's just it. I don't know. There were no labels on the bottles."

"Maybe it was raspberry juice? Or cranberry?"

"It wasn't juice at all. The liquid inside was really thick. I know this is going to sound daft, but it was almost like blood."

"Maybe Ryan is a vampire?" I laughed.

"You're right." She managed a smile. "I'm just being stupid."

"Did you ask him what it was?"

"No. I made some silly excuse, and said I had to leave."

"You need to ask him about it."

"I will. He's gone away on a course for a few days. I'll have it out with him when he gets back."

"Is the gardening business going any better than the boyfriend business?"

"Much better. In addition to the one-off jobs, I'm also starting to build up a clientele made up of customers who need regular garden maintenance. I enjoy this so much more than the modelling. There's only one slight downside, and I realise I shouldn't complain, but some customers have such bad taste."

"How do you mean?"

"The one thing that drives me crazy is people who insist on having garden gnomes. I mean, seriously? Whoever thought a garden gnome looked good?"

"Do you get many requests for gnomes?"

"A surprising number. Still, I shouldn't complain because I've sourced a really cheap supplier, so I'm making a killing on them."

***

I hadn't been in the house for more than a few minutes when Jack came home.

"You're early. I haven't started dinner yet."

"The boss let me go early because I was there so late yesterday." He held up a small flyer. "Do you fancy this?"

"What is it?"

"A guy was delivering them door-to-door. There's a new chippy opened a few streets away."

"A fish and chip shop? Yes!" I punched the air.

"I'm not sure it's all that exciting."

"Of course it is. Fish and chips? Best. Food. Ever!"

"I hope their food is better than the name of their shop."

"What is it?"

"'But Never Battered'."

"I like it."

"You would. So, what do you think? Should we give it a try?"

"Definitely. Fish, chips and mushy peas for me."

"You do realise that this doesn't count as your having made dinner, don't you? It will still be your turn tomorrow."

"That doesn't seem fair."

The leafleting campaign had obviously worked because there was a queue snaking all the way out of the door of But Never Battered.

"Come on. Let's forget it." Jack turned back.

"No. Let's wait."

"But you hate queuing!"

"What makes you say that?"

"Probably because whenever we have to queue, you always say that you hate it."

"I do not." He was right. Normally, I hated queuing for anything, but this was different. And besides, if we'd gone back home, I would have had to cook dinner.

"Look!" I pointed to the counter. "They're serving them in old newspapers, just like they used to do."

"Are they allowed to do that? It doesn't look very hygienic."

"Of course it is. The newsprint gives it added flavour."

Jack looked unconvinced.

"Hi." The woman behind the counter greeted us when we finally made it to the front of the queue.

"Hi. We love the name of your shop, don't we, Jack?"

"Err — yeah. It's very — err — good. Very funny."

"Thanks. I'm Tish, and that's my husband, Chip."

Tish and Chip? "Very good." I laughed.

"What is?"

"The made-up names. Very funny."

"No. They really are our names."

"Oh? Sorry. I thought — err — it's just that they're quite appropriate. Tish and Chip, running a fish and chip shop?"

"I suppose they are. I hadn't thought of that."

Oh boy!

"So, what can I get for you?"

"Fish, chips and mushy peas for me, please."

"Just fish and chips for me," Jack said.

"No mushy peas?" I looked at him in disbelief.

"I don't like them."

"Freak!"

Tish handed us our food; it looked and smelled delicious.

"We're also running a special offer on cushions today."

"Sorry? I must have misheard. I thought you said — "

She reached under the counter, and produced a red

cushion.

"They're five pounds each or two for eight pounds."

"Cushions?"

"We have a variety of colours and patterns."

"Err—right. They're very nice, but I think we'll just stick with the fish and chips, thanks."

Chapter 4

The next morning, I was woken at five-thirty by a stupid bird, singing its head off.

"Can't you make it stop?" I pulled the pillow over my head.

"Why would you want to do that? It's a beautiful sound." Jack went over to the window to look for the culprit. "What better way to welcome a new morning?"

"It's the middle of the night."

"Rubbish. The sun's almost up. We should take an early morning stroll."

"No chance. I'm not getting up yet."

"I think I will. The early morning air will do me the world of good."

"While you're out there, shut that bird up, would you?"

He didn't.

It continued with its incessant noise until in the end I was forced to admit defeat.

I'd showered, dressed and was in the middle of breakfast when Jack got back.

"I was beginning to think I'd have to send out a search party for you."

"I feel so much better for that walk. Do you know what I think?"

"That you'd like to make dinner every night of the week?"

"I think we should start jogging every morning."

"You can jog on if you think I'm running around the streets."

"It would do you good. You're stuck behind that desk

all day."

"Rubbish. I spend most of the day on my feet, and have you forgotten that I am the proud owner of a lifetime subscription to I-Sweat?"

"How often do you actually work out there?"

"Most days. Sometimes more than once a day."

"I never see you with any sports gear."

"Err—that's because I keep it at work."

"Doesn't it smell?"

"Mrs V washes it for me."

"You make your PA do your laundry?"

"No, of course not. It just so happens that Mrs V has some kind of laundry fetish. She practically begged me to let her do it."

Jack gave me *that* look. "I still think an early morning jog would be good for you."

"Yeah, anyway, what about those fish and chips? They were quite something, weren't they?"

"I know you're changing the subject, but yes, they were rather nice."

"I just don't get that thing they have going with the soft furnishings."

"That was rather strange. Oh well, I suppose I'd better go and grab a shower." He started for the door. "By the way, you haven't forgotten about the charity sports competition this weekend, have you?"

"What charity sports competition?"

"Don't you remember? I told you about it the other day."

"I'm pretty sure you didn't."

"I thought I had. It's an annual sports competition between Washbridge and West Chipping police forces.

We're going to give those Washbridge lads a good hiding."

"That sounds right up your street. You should enjoy it."

He was half way upstairs when he shouted, "And everyone's partner is expected to compete too."

"What? Jack? What did you just say?"

If I had one fault, it was that I was too giving. Too selfless for my own good.

What? It's true—I just hide it well.

By the time Jack left for work, I'd somehow let myself be talked into taking part in the charity sports competition. I loved that man way too much; I just couldn't say 'no' to him. Still, how bad could it be? From what Jack had told me, it was just a few silly games that no one took particularly seriously. It would probably be a good laugh.

I know. I know. Famous last words.

***

It was Mrs V's day off; Jules was busy behind her desk.

"Morning, Jules."

She looked up and smiled, but didn't speak.

"Everything okay?"

She nodded.

What was that all about? Normally, it took me all my time to shut her up. Perhaps she was having boyfriend troubles? Maybe Gilbert's bottle top obsession was getting out of hand. Whatever it was, it was probably best not to get involved.

Winky was fast asleep on the sofa; he didn't stir when I

walked in. Lying next to him was his phone.

Hmm?

Curiosity got the better of me. If I was careful, I'd be able to sneak a look at his app. I tiptoed over to the sofa, picked up the phone, and then tiptoed to my desk. On the first screen was an icon for an app called Purrbnb—that had to be the one. Winky still hadn't stirred so I clicked on the icon. As its name suggested, it was very similar to Airbnb. It allowed me to search for short-term rental properties in any part of the country. The one striking difference was that the prices were all remarkably low—ridiculously so. I didn't see how anyone could offer to rent out their rooms or houses for that kind of money.

"Do you mind?" Winky jumped onto my desk, and snatched the phone out of my hand. "Who said you could look at that?"

"Sorry. I didn't mean to."

"Oh? I suppose the phone just happened to fly across the room, and land in your hand?"

"Your app looks a lot like Airbnb."

"With one very important difference."

"Which is?"

"You've been looking at it. Surely you noticed?"

"The prices?"

"Bingo."

"I don't understand how you got people to offer their properties to rent at such low prices. They're less than half what I'd expect them to be."

"That's the genius of it."

"How did you manage it?"

"That's a trade secret. I couldn't possibly tell you that."

"I assume you take a cut from every booking?"

"Naturally."

"I'm impressed. When do you launch?"

"It went live first thing this morning. Downloads of the app are already off the scale. This time next year, I'll be rich."

"Don't forget my twenty percent cut."

"For doing what?"

"Providing office accommodation for Purrbnb, of course."

"Dream on."

"Either that, or you find somewhere else to run your new enterprise."

"Okay, then. You're a hard woman."

Mid-morning, someone knocked on my door. Winky and I exchanged a glance (in his case, a one-eyed glance). No one ever knocked on that door.

"Come in."

Jules walked into the room. "Your post." Her voice sounded rather odd.

"Thanks. Do you have a sore throat, Jules?"

She shook her head.

"Are you feeling okay?"

She nodded.

"Are you sure? You seem rather subdued."

She nodded again, and then scurried quickly out of the room.

"What's going on with that one?" Winky said.

"No idea. Maybe she's having problems with her love life?"

"Don't talk to me about 'love lives'." He sighed.

"What's wrong? Don't tell me Peggy has dumped you?"

"Of course not. It's just that she wants us to go on a double-date with her friend, Carrie, and Carrie's boyfriend, *Tom*."

"I take it you're not keen?"

"Carrie is alright, but that boyfriend of hers is a stuck-up, toffee-nosed prat."

"You're not a fan, then?"

"He's a pedigree, and he never lets up about it. He looks down his nose at moggies like me."

"Why would you care what he thinks?"

"I don't. He just does my head in. He lives in some posh gaff on the other side of town, and is always banging on about it. And then there's me, stuck in this grotty old office."

"This office isn't grotty."

"He talks to me like I'm some kind of peasant."

"I'm surprised you stand for it."

"Normally I wouldn't, but I don't think Peggy would be very impressed if I punched him."

It was almost eleven o'clock, and Jules still hadn't brought my cup of tea through, so I pressed the talk button on the intercom. "Have you forgotten my drink, Jules?"

All kinds of strange noises came back through the speaker; it sounded as though she'd dropped the intercom onto the floor. Eventually, a deep husky voice came through, "Sorry. What would you like?"

"My usual."

"I can't remember what that is?"

Oh boy!

"Tea, please."

"Milk and sugar?"

"Milk and my usual sugar, please."

"Okay."

Five minutes later, Jules appeared, cup of tea in hand. And then something remarkable happened: she didn't spill a drop.

"Thank you." I took a sip, and almost spat it out. "How much sugar did you put in here?"

"Three teaspoons."

"What? Why would you do that?"

And then the penny dropped: The bowed head, the strange voice, the knocking on the door, and the unspilled tea.

"Lules? Is that you?"

She looked up. "I'm sorry, Jill."

"What's going on? Where is Jules?"

Lules pulled off her wig. "Jules has been poorly all night."

"And she asked you to stand in for her?"

"No! She doesn't know anything about it. Jules asked me to phone and tell you she couldn't make it, but I thought it would be a good chance to get some experience. You won't tell Jules, will you? She'll kill me."

"I won't tell her. What about your job at the black pudding factory?"

"I called in sick. I couldn't miss out on this opportunity. I'm really sorry. I suppose I'd better go."

"Hold on. If it means that much to you, you can stay for the rest of the day. But don't touch anything on the computer. Just sit out there, and greet any visitors. Okay?"

"Yeah. Thanks, Jill."

"One more thing, Lules." I passed her a slip of paper.

"That's the number for my next-door neighbour, Megan Lovemore. She's worked in the modelling business for some time. She said if you give her a call, she'd be happy to talk to you."

"That's brill! Thank you so much, Jill. Jules was right about you."

"She most certainly was right about you," Winky said, after Lules had gone back to the outer office. "You're such a soft touch."

***

Ever since Desdemona Nightowl's visit, I'd been eager to find out more about the portrait that she'd given to me. Not only the portrait, but also the pendant. I had so many questions: Who was the woman in the picture? Who was the man with the red hair and red beard? To find all the answers, I would probably have to return to CASS. In the meantime, I intended to try to find out more about the pendant, so I called in at the antique jeweller that was located on one of the side roads, off the high street.

Some of the letters on the sign must have dropped off because instead of reading 'Antique Jewellery' it now read 'Ant Jewellery', which conjured up some amusing images in my mind.

"Good morning!" A jovial, old wizard with huge sideburns stood behind the counter.

"Morning. You seem to have lost a few letters from your sign."

"Really? It must have been that strong wind last night." He came out from behind the counter, and went outside to take a look. "It looks okay to me."

"Shouldn't it say, 'Antique Jewellery'?"

"Now I understand your confusion." He laughed. "I'm Anthony Coultard, but everyone calls me Ant. Hence the name of the shop."

"I see. Sorry to have worried you like that."

"No problem at all. It's nice to have a witch in the shop. I don't get many sups in here. How can I be of assistance?"

"Would you take a look at this pendant, please." I put it on the counter.

"Are you wanting to sell it?"

"No. I wondered if you might be able to give me any idea how old it is?"

He picked it up and studied it closely. "Interesting. Very interesting. You called it a pendant, I believe?"

"Yes?"

"Actually, it's a locket."

"Really? Are you sure?" I'd studied the pendant many times, and I'd seen nothing to indicate that it was anything but a solid piece of jewellery.

"This is not from the human world, but you probably already know that. I've only ever seen one similar piece before, and that was many centuries ago."

"I can't see any way to open it."

"You won't. It's been sealed by magic."

"Do you know how to open it?"

"Yes and no."

"Sorry. I don't follow."

"I know the spell required to open a locket such as this, but I doubt my magic is strong enough to do the trick. The only other one I've seen was opened by one of the most powerful wizards in Candlefield—he's long dead now."

"If you can show me the spell, I might be able to open it."

"Hmm? I think that's unlikely."

"I'd like to try."

"Wait here, then. It might take me a few minutes to find it." He disappeared into the back of the shop.

While he was gone, I took a look around. There were some beautiful pieces. One ring in particular caught my eye, but the price was eye-watering. Maybe I should ask Jack to buy it for me to celebrate our 'anniversary'.

"Here you are." He reappeared clutching several sheets of paper. "I was beginning to think I might have thrown it away by mistake."

"Thank you." I began to study the spell.

"I'm sorry. I didn't catch your name."

"Jill. Jill Gooder."

"Oh my. I'm so sorry. I didn't—err—that's to say—I had no idea. In that case, you should be able to open it if anyone can."

I focussed on the locket and cast the spell.

"You did it!" Ant exclaimed. "Do you know them?"

"No, I don't."

Inside the locket was a picture of a man with red hair and a red beard, and a young woman with long, dark hair. It was the same woman who appeared in the portrait that Desdemona Nightowl had given to me.

"They're not relatives of yours, then?"

"No. I have no idea who they are, but I intend to find out."

Chapter 5

As I was already near to the high street, I decided to pay a visit to WashBets. If anyone was keeping a check on me, they would probably think I had some kind of gambling addiction because I seemed to spend almost as much time in there as in my own office.

Tonya (AKA the mathematical genius) was behind the counter again, looking even more dead inside than usual.

"I'd like to speak to Ryan, please."

"If it's a complaint, you need to speak to his assistant, Bryan."

"Don't you remember me?"

"Are you his girlfriend?"

This was becoming more and more like Groundhog Day.

"I'm not his girlfriend. I need to speak to him about Megan."

"Is that you?"

"No. That's his girlfriend."

"I thought you said you weren't his girlfriend?"

"I'm not, and I wasn't the other two times I was in here. Please just tell him that Jill is here to talk to him about Megan."

"Does he have *two* girlfriends now?"

Beam me up, someone, please.

"Hi, Jill." Ryan greeted me when I'd finally managed to get past the enigma that was Tonya.

"I can't keep doing this, Ryan. That woman is slowly wearing me down."

"Who? Megan?"

"No, not Megan. Tonya. She's driving me potty."

"Is Megan okay?"

"Not really. She's freaked out by the bottles of red liquid in your fridge."

"Oh no." He put his hand to his mouth.

"Oh yes. What were you thinking?"

"I wasn't. It never occurred to me that she might look in there. I thought it was strange when she rushed off the other day."

"Megan told me she thought it was blood."

"What did you say?"

"I told her you must be a vampire."

"You did what?" He looked horrified.

"Relax. She thought I was joking. What did you expect?"

"I'll hide the bottles."

"It's too late for that. She's already seen them. You'll have to come up with some kind of explanation before you see her next."

"Like what?"

"I don't know. Tell her it's an iron supplement that you have to take."

"Do you think she'll buy that?"

"I don't see why not. I can't think of anything better."

"Okay, I'll do that. Thanks, Jill."

"Please make sure you don't do any more stupid things, like turning into a bat in front of her. I don't think I could bear another session with the Tonya-bot."

***

I'd read through all the newspaper clippings in the box

file that Sophie Brownling had left with me. The articles, which had been published at the time of her daughter's disappearance, all pretty much mirrored one another: Four girls had gone out to celebrate a birthday; only three had made it back home.

Following an appeal on local TV by Sophie Brownling and her husband, there had been several apparent 'sightings' of Angie, but they had all come to nothing. In the years that followed, the number of newspaper articles had gradually decreased. The only stories that had appeared in the press during the last few years had been small articles published on the anniversary of Angie's disappearance.

The internet offered little by way of additional information because Net usage was much less back then than it is today. Unlike now, there was precious little social media to jump on every story.

My next port of call was Washbridge Library. Maybe there would be other articles in the newspaper archives that might help.

"Is Mad in?" I asked the grim-faced woman behind reception.

"Who?"

"Madeline Lane?"

"Oh, her? Yes, she's on a break. *Again*."

"Any idea where I'll find her?"

"She usually goes into the garden around the back. If she's there, remind her that her break finished ten minutes ago, would you?"

"Sure."

Mad was lying on a bench next to the rose beds, and if I

wasn't mistaken, she was fast asleep.

"Wakey, wakey!"

She jumped so much that she almost tumbled off the bench.

"Jill? You scared me to death."

"Sorry to disturb your beauty sleep."

She checked her watch. "Oh no. I'm in trouble."

"The woman on reception said I should tell you that your break finished ten minutes ago."

"That's Rhoda. She's my new boss, and a real battle-axe. I'm telling you, Jill, I've just about had it with this place."

"Are you thinking of packing in the library job?"

"It isn't just the library. I'm fed up with Washbridge. There's nothing to do; the nightlife is practically non-existent."

"I thought you had no option but to stay here?"

"That was true when I first took the ghost hunting job, but I have more experience now, so I get a bit more say in what I do. I've applied for a post in London. If I get it, I'll be able to tell them what to do with their library job."

"I'd be sorry to see you go."

"You could come and visit me. We could have some cracking nights out down there."

"I'm a bit old for all that."

"Don't be soft. You're not past it quite yet."

Quite?

"When will you know if you've got the new job?"

"It'll be a while yet. Do me a favour, would you? Don't mention any of this to my mum if you see her."

"Deli won't be very happy if you leave Washbridge."

"She and Nails are one of the reasons that I have to get out of this place."

"Are they still together?"

"Yeah, but for how long is anybody's guess. He's driving everyone batty with those bottle tops."

"Is he still going to the Toppers Anonymous meetings?"

"Yeah. He daren't pack those in, or Mum would kick him out again. That doesn't stop him from rattling on all day about the bottle tops he already owns. It drives me mad; I just want to get in his face and shout: No one cares! They're just bottle tops!"

Mad may not have liked her job in the library, but she was a whizz with the microfiche. It was just as well because I never had got to grips with those infernal machines.

We found numerous articles on Angie's disappearance, but they were the same ones I'd already read from the clippings provided by Sophie Brownling.

"Have you seen this article?" Mad pointed to the screen.

I hadn't, but that was because the article related to the abduction and murder of a young woman named Patty Lake. That had taken place about nine months after Angie Potts had disappeared. A man named Conrad Landers had been arrested and charged with her murder. The reason Mad had pointed it out was because the last line of the article suggested that the police were going to question him about Angie Potts' disappearance too.

"Interesting." I turned to Mad. "Are you okay to help me for a little longer?"

"Sure. Anything to save me from Rhoda."

"Let's see what else we can find out about the Patty Lake case."

And that's what we did for the next forty minutes. Nothing came of Conrad Landers' supposed connection to the Angie Potts disappearance. He was eventually convicted of the murder of Patty Lake, and sentenced to life imprisonment. According to an article that covered the trial, he was still protesting his innocence as he was taken out of court to begin his sentence.

"Thanks Mad. I appreciate the help."

"No problem. Do you have to rush off?"

"Not really. Why?"

"I thought we could nip over to GT, and grab a coffee in Spooky Wooky."

"What about your boss?"

"She's not invited."

***

Harry and Larry were behind the counter in Spooky Wooky.

"If it isn't two of our favourite ladies," Harry greeted us. "I know Jill will want a blueberry muffin, but what about you, Mad?"

"I'll have the same. And a cup of green tea, please."

"Green tea?" I gave Mad a sour look. "Since when did you drink green tea?"

"I love it. I can't get enough of the stuff."

Freak!

"I'll have a caramel latte, please, Harry."

"Why don't you ladies find a table, and I'll bring it over?"

"I don't receive this kind of service in Cuppy C," I said, as we took a seat at a table next to the jukebox.

"This isn't the norm. It must be because you're GT's new celebrity."

"Don't say that."

"It's true. You're the talk of Ghost Town."

"Great! That's just what I need."

Mad and I chatted for a while, and were just about to leave when Harry and Larry approached our table.

"Could we have a word before you go, Jill?" Larry said.

"Sure."

"I'd better make tracks." Mad stood up. "Good luck with the missing person case, Jill."

"Thanks. Keep me posted on the London situation."

"Will do."

Harry and Larry took a seat at my table. A young man with curly ginger hair was now holding the fort behind the counter.

"Thanks for sparing us some time," Harry said. "We know how busy you are."

"No problem. What's on your mind?"

"Before we opened Spooky Wooky, we used to run a small bakery in the human world. Until the fire, that is."

"So I heard."

"Did you also hear that foul play was involved?"

"Yes. Constance mentioned that it may have been arson."

"There's no 'may' about it." Larry jumped in. "It was murder—plain and simple."

"Did they ever get anyone?"

"The police?" Harry scoffed. "Those useless idiots didn't do a thing. They said it was an accident."

"Could it have been?"

"Not a chance."

"Do you have any idea who might have done it?"

"More than an idea," Harry said. "We know exactly

who did it. It was Stewey Dewey. He was one of our competitors. Once we were out of the way, there was nothing to stop him from taking all of our customers."

"Where was your bakery?"

"In Washbridge. Do you know Deerstalker Lane?"

"Is that near the hospital?"

"Yes. Just down the road from there."

"What exactly would you like me to do?"

"We want justice, Jill," Harry said. "We want Dewey behind bars. Will you help us?"

"How long ago was the fire?"

"Five years now."

"It might be difficult after all that time, but I'll see what I can do."

"Thank you." Harry leaned over and gave me a hug.

"I know this is a little cheeky," Larry said. "But could we ask another small favour?"

"What's that?"

"We're always on the lookout for ways to improve this place, but we've kind of lost touch with what's going on in the human world. We thought you might have some ideas that we could use?"

"Not really, but what might help would be for you to come and see my favourite coffee shop in Washbridge. It's called Coffee Triangle, and they have some pretty unusual ideas."

"That would be great," Harry said.

"Why don't you both join me the next time I go there. You can take a look around, and see if anything inspires you?"

"That sounds like a plan."

While I'd been talking to Harry and Larry, the colonel and Priscilla had taken a table nearby.

"Hello, you two. I didn't expect to see you here in GT."

"We could say the same about you." The colonel grinned. "Won't you join us? I'll get you a drink."

"I'm sorry, but I can't. I've already been here much longer than I intended. How are things at the house?"

"They're fine."

"You don't sound very sure. Are you having problems again?"

"No, nothing like that. It's just that we've been doing a lot of thinking lately, haven't we, Cilla?"

She nodded. "Briggsy and I have decided that it's wrong for us to cling onto the human world."

"Does that mean you're going to vacate the house, and move to GT?"

"Goodness, no," the colonel said. "Not completely. We're going to look for somewhere to live over here. That way we'll be able to split our time between the house and GT."

"I see. Have you found anywhere suitable?"

"No, but then we haven't told you all of our plans yet."

"Go on."

"Neither of us likes the idea of kicking our heels all day long. We thought we might like to run a small business of some kind—a shop or maybe even a tea room like this one. Ideally, we'd like to find one with living accommodation included."

"I can see you've given this a lot of thought. It all sounds very exciting."

"We think so."

"Well, good luck with it all. Keep me posted on how

you get on."

As soon as I stepped out of the coffee shop, I heard raised voices—voices that I recognised. A few yards down the street, my mother and father were going at it hammer and tongs.

"Do you seriously expect me to believe that?" my mother yelled.

"You can believe whatever you want. You usually do!"

"Hey, you two!" I stood in between them before they came to blows. "What's going on?"

"Ask this thief." My mother was red in the face, and clearly ready to set about my father.

"I haven't stolen anything. I've told you a thousand times that I didn't put them there."

"Pull the other one!"

"Whoa! Stop it, both of you. Mum, will you please tell me what this is all about?"

"I'll be glad to. This morning when we got up, Alberto noticed that two of his garden gnomes were missing. Your father has always taken great pleasure in mocking Alberto's collection, so I suspected he might have something to do with it. And sure enough, where did I find them? Behind his garden shed." She pointed an accusatory finger.

"I've told your mother that I didn't put them there."

"I suppose they walked there by themselves, did they?"

"Mum! Let Dad have his say."

"Thank you, Jill. As I was trying to say, the first I knew about it was when your mother came hammering on our door."

"Seriously? Is that the best you can come up with?" She

turned to me. "You're a P.I, Jill. You must recognise a cock-and-bull story when you hear one?"

"The first thing I learned in this business was never to jump to conclusions."

"Absolutely." My father grinned.

My mother scowled but said nothing.

"If you two will promise to call a truce, I will undertake to find out what really happened. If I discover Dad was behind this, then you can give him what for, and I won't stand in your way. But if I discover Dad wasn't responsible, then you'll have to apologise to him. Do you both agree?"

"I agree." My father grinned.

My mother mumbled something under her breath.

"Mum?"

"Okay, but it's a waste of your time. You're bound to find out he did it."

"Mum!"

"Okay. I agree."

Chapter 6

When I got back to the office, Lules was looking very pleased with herself.

"Is everything okay, Lules? Any messages?"

"Everything's fine. There was just one phone call. Someone wanted to make an appointment to see you this afternoon. I checked your diary, and could see you were free, so I've booked her in."

"Who was it?"

"I'm not absolutely sure because the line wasn't very good, but I think she said her name was Polly."

"And did Polly say what it was about?"

"She said she had a job for you. That's good, isn't it?"

"Very good. What time is she coming in?"

"At three-thirty."

"Well done, Lules."

"Thanks." She beamed with obvious pride.

Another new client, eh? The way things were shaping up, this was going to be a really profitable month. Luther would be proud of me.

There were two other cats in my office.

"Do you want the monthly plan or would you prefer to pay for the year?" Winky asked the first in line.

"How much would I save with the annual plan?" The Siamese enquired.

"It's fifteen pounds per month or one-hundred and forty-four for the year. A saving of twenty percent."

The Siamese gave it some thought. "Just stick me down for the monthly."

Winky gave the Siamese a membership card, and then

went on to serve the Burmese, who opted for the annual plan.

"You're heading for a fall," I said, after the two cats had left via the window.

"What are you banging on about now?"

"I assume you're still selling membership to Moonlight Gym?"

"Yeah. What of it?"

"I told you that the I-Sweat boys have had CCTV cameras installed. You're going to get caught out."

"Let me worry about that. You worry about your own business." He smirked. "If you can call it that."

I couldn't understand how he could be so blasé. He didn't seem the least bit concerned that his illegal gym operation might get busted. Why not? What did he know that I didn't?

While I waited for my new client to arrive, I busied myself re-reading the newspaper clippings related to the Angie Potts case.

At three-thirty on the dot, I heard the outer door open — my new client, no doubt. Moments later, Lules came through to my office.

"She's here, Jill."

"Okay. Show her in."

"Just one thing. I must have misheard her name. It's not Polly. It's actually Lolly."

Oh no!

"Jill!" Lolly Jolly burst into the room. "Thank you for seeing me at such short notice."

"Lolly. It's you."

"In the flesh. Can I get a drink? I'm parched."

"Sure. Tea? Coffee?"

"Don't you have any of the hard stuff?"

"Sorry, no. It's just tea or coffee, I'm afraid."

"I'll have coffee, then. Milk, no sugar."

"And I'll have a tea, please, Lules."

"I didn't expect to see you again so soon, Lolly," I said, through gritted teeth, once Lules had brought our drinks.

"It's so great that we've all been reunited. I had a really good time with you and Kathy, the other day."

"So did we. I'd love to do it more often, but I'm always so busy. Kathy has lots of time on her hands, though. You should give her a call, sometime."

Revenge was so sweet. Snigger.

"I'll do that. Anyway, I wanted to see you because I need your professional help."

"Oh?"

"I didn't like to say anything before because I was embarrassed, but the real reason I moved back to Washbridge was to get away from my ex-boyfriend."

"What happened?"

"The relationship didn't work out, but he wouldn't accept it. He started to follow me, and even turned up at my place of work a couple of times. In the end, I decided the best thing to do would be to move away from him altogether, so I came back home."

"That makes sense."

"The trouble is that he's followed me. I've seen him a couple of times now. He hasn't actually approached me, but it was definitely him. It's kind of creeping me out."

"I'm not surprised. Have you thought of going to the police?"

"The problem is that he's originally from around here too, so before I can go to the police, I need proof that he came back with the intention of following me. That's where you come in."

"What exactly do you want me to do?"

"Keep an eye on him. Follow him for a while to see what he does."

"How will I know him?"

"His name is Nick Long. I can email you a photo of him. He's renting a bedsit in Westcliff House. It's a real dump."

"How do you know where he's living?"

"I — err — saw him coming out of the building."

"Are you sure he's following you?"

"Why else would he be up here?"

"I normally ask for a retainer of three hundred pounds, if that's okay."

"That's fine." She opened her handbag. "Oh, dash it. Wouldn't you just know. I've left my purse at home. I'll get the cash to you later, if that's okay?"

Thankfully, Lolly had an appointment with her hairdresser so she couldn't stay long. What a piece of work she was. My chances of ever getting paid for working on her case were practically nil, but I had thought of a way to keep my costs to a minimum.

"Winky, I have a job for your crew."

"What are you talking about?"

"Don't you remember? In return for me keeping silent on your Moonlight Gym scam, you promised that you'd make your crew available to carry out surveillance for me."

"Did I say that?"

"Do I really need to play back the conversation on the

digital recorder?"

"That won't be necessary. What do you need them to do?"

"I want them to keep an eye on Lolly Jolly's boyfriend."

"Is that the ditsy woman who just left? The one with the bad taste in clothes?"

"Yeah. Her boyfriend is living in Westcliff House. I'll email you his photo as soon as she sends it to me. I want to know if he goes anywhere near Lolly."

"Okay. I'll get my guys on it."

What about that for cost cutting? Luther would be proud of me.

***

The outer door crashed open, and I heard Lules shout, 'You can't go in there!'.

Moments later, Grandma came charging into my office.

"Sorry, Jill," Lules said. "I did try to stop her."

"It's okay, Lules. I can take care of this."

"I think you're losing the plot, Jill," Grandma said.

"Sorry?"

"Even I know your PA is called Jules. You just called her Lules."

"That *is* Lules. Well, Lulu actually. She's Jules' sister."

"If you say so. Now, what do you know about YarnStormers?"

Oh bum!

"Who?"

"I've heard on the woolvine that someone called YarnStormers is going to open a shop here in Washbridge. What do you know about it?"

"Nothing," I lied. "Why would I? I've never even heard of them."

"What good is it having a granddaughter as a P.I. if she doesn't know anything?"

"I'm not sure you understand what being a P.I. means."

"Apparently, it means not knowing information of vital importance to my business. You'd better do some sniffing around. If they do intend to move in on my territory, I need to be forewarned. And do you know why?"

"Because forewarned is forearmed?"

"Exactly. If they think they can muscle in on me, they have another think coming."

"Okay, Grandma. I'll see if I can find out anything about them."

"While I'm here, there's something else I wanted to speak to you about."

Oh goody.

"There's a sponsored bike ride in Candlefield on Sunday in aid of the Aged Witches Society."

"Are you a member of the Aged Witches whatsit?"

"Do I look like an aged witch?"

"Err — well — you are — err — "

"I am what?"

"Nothing. It sounds like a very good cause. Do you know someone who is taking part in it?"

"Me, of course."

"You?" I laughed. "Ride a bike?"

"And, why wouldn't I?"

"Err — no reason, I guess. Sorry. I'd be delighted to sponsor you. Do you have the form with you?"

"I didn't come here to ask you to sponsor me."

"You didn't? Then I'm confused."

"I came here to inform you that you'll be my partner on Sunday."

"What do you mean? Partner?"

"Didn't I mention it? It's a tandem bike ride."

"Me? Ride a bike? No way!"

"But you said yourself that it's for a good cause."

"That was before I knew you wanted to get me on a bike."

"I've put your name down already."

"I'm not fit enough to ride a bike for any distance."

"Your sister told me that you work out at the gym every day. That's why I thought of you."

"She might have misunderstood what I said."

"That's settled then. I'll see you in Candlefield market square on Sunday at two pm. Don't be late. And let me know as soon as you have the lowdown on YarnStormers."

As soon as she was out of the door, I made a call to Kathy.

"Grandma knows about YarnStormers."

"What do you mean? Does she know they've offered me a job? You didn't tell her, did you?"

"Of course I didn't. What do you take me for? She doesn't know about your job offer, but she has heard that they may be opening a shop in Washbridge."

"What did she say about it?"

"She wasn't best pleased, as you can imagine. She wants me to find out what their plans are."

"Are you going to tell her that they're moving in across the road?"

"I'm not going to tell her anything. I'll just act stupid,

and make out that I couldn't find any information."

"She'll kill me if I decide to take the job."

"Still not made your mind up, then?"

"Not yet. Hold on, I can see her coming down the street. I'd better go. Thanks for the tip-off."

***

All the way home, I was trying to figure out how I could get out of the sponsored tandem ride, but so far, I'd drawn a blank. There would be no point in feigning injury because even if I turned up with my leg in plaster, Grandma would still expect me to go ahead with it. It was a pity Jack wasn't a sup; he'd definitely be up for taking part.

I couldn't pull onto my driveway because it was blocked by Bessie, Mr Hosey's silly train. The man himself was standing next to it; he appeared to be having a shouting match with Mr Kilbride.

"I can't take any more!" Hosey yelled.

"You knew what you were getting into!" Kilbride fired back.

"Yes, but I didn't expect you to be doing it all the time. It's giving me a migraine."

"Either you honour the agreement, or I want my money back."

"You can whistle for that!"

I thought for a moment that Kilbride was going to set about Mr Hosey, but instead he stormed off across the road, and disappeared into his house.

"I'm sorry you had to witness that, Jill." Mr Hosey

sighed. "There is no reasoning with that man."

"What's the problem?"

"He insists on playing those stupid bagpipes every moment he's on the train. There's a limit to what a person can stand."

"He didn't seem very happy."

"That's his problem. I don't mind him playing them say once a day. But I'm not prepared to listen to them morning, noon and night. Anyway, I'd better get Bessie out of your way."

Once he'd moved the train, I pulled onto the driveway. The bin was still at the front of the house because it had been emptied earlier that day. I wheeled it around the back, and was just about to let myself into the house when two terrifying creatures came around the corner. The giant ants were standing upright on two legs, and were coming straight at me. What kind of evil magic was this? Was Ma Chivers behind it?

I had to act quickly or I'd be ant food.

I cast the 'smaller' spell, and made them normal ant size. I was just about to stamp on them when I heard a squeak. It sounded like a tiny voice, and it was coming from one of the ants. I dropped down onto my knees, and listened.

"Jill! Don't stamp on us!" said the squeaky voice.

"It's us, Tony and Clare," said the second squeaky voice.

Oh no. I'd shrunk my cosplay-loving neighbours. And even worse, I'd almost squished them.

"Help us, Jill!"

I quickly reversed the 'smaller' spell, and then cast the

'forget' spell.

"Hi, Tony. Hi, Clare. I like your costumes."

"Err—thanks. Sorry, I just went a little light-headed." Tony shook his ant-head.

"We're going to AntCon this weekend," Clare said. "Would you and Jack like to join us?"

"We'd love to, but we're already fully booked. Maybe next time."

Chapter 7

I'd made myself scrambled eggs on toast for breakfast; Jack was still trying to decide between muesli and porridge.

"We should get in some practice tonight," he said.

"Practice for what?"

"The charity sports competition."

"I thought you said it was all just light-hearted fun."

"It is, but that doesn't mean I don't want to win."

"Not everything has to be a competition."

"Do we have any sacks?"

"No. Santa took them all."

"Pity. We could have practised the sack race."

"If you think I'm jumping up and down inside a sack, you have another think coming."

"We have eggs. If we hard-boil a couple, we could practise the egg and spoon race."

"In our back garden?"

"Why not?"

"Because the neighbours will think we've lost our minds."

"Speaking of the neighbours." Jack had finally opted for the porridge. "I forgot to mention last night that I saw Tony and Clare. They were dressed as ants. They looked kind of cool."

"Don't you think it would be nice to have normal neighbours?"

"Tony and Clare are okay. Apparently, it's AntCon this Sunday. It's a pity that we have the charity sports competition, or I would have liked to go."

"To AntCon? Why would you want to dress up as an

ant?"

"I must admit, I'd prefer to be a spider; they're much cooler. I wonder if there's a SpiderCon?"

"Sadly, I suspect there probably is."

***

Not long after Jack had left for work, I had a phone call from Aunt Lucy.

"I'm sorry to trouble you so early, Jill."

"That's okay. Is something wrong?"

"It's Barry. He — err — well — err"

"Is he ill? Has he been hurt?"

"No, nothing like that. I don't know what's wrong with him; he won't say. He seems really down, and he won't go out in the garden. I know you're busy, but if you could spare a few minutes, I thought you might be able to get him to talk to you about it."

"I'll come straight over."

Aunt Lucy was right; Barry wasn't his usual bubbly self. Normally when I went to visit, he was all over me. Today, though, he was curled up under the table in the dining room.

"See what I mean?" Aunt Lucy whispered.

"Yeah. It might be best if you let me talk to him alone."

"Okay. Good luck."

I got down on all-fours and crawled over to the table.

"Hi, Barry."

"Hello." He couldn't have looked more sorry for himself if he'd tried.

"What's wrong, big guy?"

"Nothing."

"Come on. I can see there's something the matter. Aren't you feeling well?"

"I feel okay."

"What is it, then?"

"You'll laugh."

"I won't laugh. I promise."

"Do you swear on your blueberry muffins?"

Sheesh, even the dog was at it now. "Yes, I swear on my blueberry muffins that I won't laugh."

"A cat is being nasty to me."

"A cat?" I almost laughed, but managed to check myself just in time. "What do you mean by *nasty*?"

"Every time I go out into the garden, he attacks me. Last time I went out there, he scratched me on my nose." Barry pointed with his paw.

It was only when I got up close that I could see the minutest of scratches. "That looks sore."

"It is. He's really mean, and I didn't do anything. I just wanted to be his friend."

"Do you know where he lives?"

"In one of the gardens that backs onto this house."

"Will you show me?"

Barry got to his feet, walked over to the window, and jumped up so his two front paws were on the window sill. "That house there."

"And you say he comes after you every time you go into the garden?"

"Yeah. I don't want to go out there again."

"What colour is this cat?"

"Ginger with a white face."

"Okay, Barry. You stay here. I'll be right back."

"What's wrong with him?" Aunt Lucy was waiting outside the door.

I gestured that we should go through to the kitchen.

"He's being bullied."

"Who by?"

"The cat who lives in the house behind yours."

"By a cat?"

"I know. You'd think that big lump would be able to look after himself, but he's clearly terrified."

"What can we do?"

"I'm going to sort it out. You wait here."

I opened the back door, but before stepping out, I cast a spell to turn myself into a Barry lookalike. It was kind of freaky to find myself inside the body of a big, soft dog. Could I bark, I wondered? I gave it a try, and sure enough, I was barking like a good 'un. So much so that a couple of dogs in the neighbourhood barked back at me. But it wasn't other dogs I was interested in. I had an appointment with a bully of a cat.

I wandered around the garden a few times, sniffing the flower beds. I'd never realised just how sensitive a dog's nose was.

"Hello, Ugly Boy!"

I looked up to see a ginger cat sitting on the fence. I ignored him, and went back to sniffing the flowers.

"What did I tell you, Ugly Boy? This garden belongs to me. You'd better get back inside before your nose gets another whacking."

What a nasty piece of work that cat was. I was going to enjoy this.

"This is my garden." I met the cat's gaze. "I can walk around it if I want to."

"See, that's where you're wrong." He jumped off the fence. "I guess I'm going to have to teach you another lesson."

The next thing I knew, the cat was rushing towards me. It was about to slash me with its claws when I swiped it with my front paw. The force of the blow sent the cat spiralling into a bush.

Dazed, it got back to its feet. "Now you're dead, Ugly Boy." It charged at me again. This time I sent it flying into the flower bed.

It took him longer to get to his feet this time. He was clearly shaken from the blows, but even more confused by what had just happened.

"Get out of my garden, you smelly cat. If you come in here again, I'll give you much worse than that."

The cat hesitated for a moment, but then jumped onto the fence and over into the garden beyond.

Job done.

"Well done, Jill," Aunt Lucy patted me on the back after I'd reversed the spell.

"I don't think Barry will have any more problems with that little monster. I'll go and give him the good news."

I found him back under the table.

"Barry. You can go into the garden now."

"What about that horrible cat?"

"I've had a word with him, and he said he won't give you any more trouble."

"Honestly?"

"I promise."

"What if he's lying?"

"He isn't. It's perfectly safe. Why don't you have a run out there now while I watch you?"

"Okay. If you're sure it's safe."

"It is. I promise."

Barry made his way cautiously into the garden. Once outside, he looked over at the back fence.

"It's okay, Barry. He won't give you any more trouble."

Barry edged around the garden—slowly at first, but then as he became more confident, he began to run around and around in circles.

"Thank you, Jill!"

"It was my pleasure."

***

After that little episode, I decided to reward myself with a muffin.

What? It was the very least I deserved.

When I arrived at Cuppy C, one of the assistants was behind the counter. The twins were busy at the far side of the shop; they had a tape-measure stretched between them, and Pearl was scribbling down notes.

"What are they up to?" I asked the assistant, as she made my coffee.

"Your guess is as good as mine. They never tell us anything."

Armed with my drink and muffin, I took a table as close to the twins as I could get.

"Measuring for another serving hatch?"

They both shot me a death-glare.

"Sorry, sorry. Just my little joke. What are you up to?"

"We're going to have a fish tank in here. We're just making sure we know how much room we have for it."

"What inspired that idea?"

"I had to go to the dentist last week." Amber held her jaw. "I'd lost a filling."

"Ouch. Is it okay now?"

"Yes. All sorted. They have a fish tank in the waiting room. That got me thinking that it would add to the ambience in here."

"That's not a bad idea."

The twins exchanged a shocked look.

"Did you hear that, Pearl? Jill thinks we've had a good idea."

"I know. Colour me shocked."

"Okay, okay. I know I'm sometimes down on your ideas."

"*Sometimes?*" Amber rolled her eyes. "You're always Debbie Downer. Isn't she, Pearl?"

"Yeah. All the time."

"I'm sorry. I don't mean to be. It's just that I don't like to see you make mistakes that might damage the shop's reputation, or cost you money. But the fish tank is a great idea. When will you get it?"

"Next week, hopefully. We don't want it before then because we need as much room as possible for the book signing evening."

"Oh yeah. I'd forgotten all about Tammy what's-her-face."

"Winestock."

"That's her. Is that still happening, then?"

"You bet. It's a real coup for us to get her. There's been a ton of interest. This place will be choc-a-bloc."

I had to hand it to the twins. After more than their fair share of duds, they had now come up with two winners. The fish in Bar Fish had proven to be very popular before they were replaced by piranhas. And, although I'd never heard of Tammy Winestock, it seemed likely that she would pull in the crowds.

***

Mrs V was by herself in the office; she was thoroughly engrossed in research for her family tree. Once again, she had her paperwork spread out over the two desks.

"Morning, Mrs V. I see you're still at it."

"Yes, dear. I never realised that genealogy could be so exciting."

"Have you found any skeletons in the cupboard?"

"How do you mean, dear?"

"Any scoundrels in the family. Black sheep—that kind of thing?"

"Nothing like that, thank goodness, but I have discovered that one of my ancestors, a man named Tobias Fotheringham, was a factory owner right here in Washbridge."

"Really? Which factory?"

"Do you remember the old sock factory?"

"I know the building you mean. It's been converted into apartments. In fact, a friend of mine lives there."

"That's the one. Do you think your friend might allow me to visit the building? I'd love to be able to stand in the spot where my ancestor once worked."

"I don't know, but I can certainly ask. Oh, and before I

forget, a friend of my aunt is moving to Washbridge soon. She's an avid knitter, and was hoping to meet other yarnies. Would you mind if I give her your contact details?"

"Not at all. She's more than welcome to join our little group. What's her name?"

"I can't remember. Oh, wait a minute. Biddy, that was it."

"Why can I smell dog on you?" Winky jumped onto my desk.

"I had to turn myself into a dog."

"You did what? Why?"

"My aunt's dog was having problems with a cat. It was bullying him."

"What kind of wussy dog is it that lets a cat bully him?"

"Barry isn't a wuss. He's just very sensitive."

"So, dog-lady, what did you get up to? Did you go around sniffing bums?"

"Don't be disgusting. If you must know, I put the bully in his place."

"Oh charming. So now I find out that I'm sharing an office with a cat beater."

"I'm not a cat beater. I just defended myself. I don't think that cat will be bothering Barry again."

"If you can change yourself into a dog, does that mean you could change yourself into a cat?"

"I don't know. I suppose so."

"You should give it a go, and then we could fool around a little."

Someone please erase that image from my mind.

Chapter 8

It was no good, I needed to start working out regularly. It's not like I had any excuses: the gym was literally next door, and I had the free life-time membership.

"Jill?" Brent was on reception at I-Sweat.

"You don't have to look quite so surprised to see me."

"Sorry. You've picked a good time; it's very quiet in there at the moment. George is in the gym if you need any help."

"Thanks."

Once I'd changed, I found George, tinkering with one of the CCTV cameras that had been installed since I was last in there.

"Jill? Long time, no see."

"How is the CCTV working out?"

"I'm beginning to think it was a waste of money."

"Really? Isn't it working?"

"It's working fine, but it isn't helping to solve the mystery of the animal fur."

"How come?"

"We've had it running for a while now. We check it first thing every morning, but so far, it hasn't captured anything unusual, and yet we're still finding animal fur on the equipment every day. It doesn't make any sense."

He was right; it didn't make any sense. Winky was still running his illegal Moonlight Gym operation, so why hadn't the CCTV caught him at it? And why hadn't Winky been more concerned when I'd told him that the cameras were being installed? I was definitely missing something.

"Do you think I could take a look at your CCTV set-up when I've finished my workout, George?"

"Sure, but why?"

"Between you and me, I'm a bit of a CCTV anorak. You won't tell anyone, will you?"

"Your secret is safe with me." He grinned. "Come and find me when you've finished your workout, and I'll take you to the 'control centre'."

"Control Centre?"

"It sounds better than saying the broom cupboard. That's where we have it set up."

"Right. Got it."

Whose stupid idea was this workout? I was holding onto the rail of the treadmill that I'd just stepped off. I daren't let go because my legs had turned to jelly.

"Are you okay, Jill?" George appeared at my side.

"Yeah! Brilliant!"

"Are you sure?"

"Couldn't be better."

"Have you tried our new cross-trainer?"

"Not yet."

"You should. It's state of the art."

"Right. I'll give it a go in a minute."

I waited until he'd walked away, and then crawled out of the gym on all-fours.

By the time I'd showered and dressed, I was feeling slightly more human, even though I was still walking like a crab with arthritis.

"That was a short session," George said when I caught up with him.

"Short, but high-intensity. That's the way I like it."

"Do you still want to take a look at our CCTV set-up?"
"Is the cupboard far from here?"
"Just down the corridor."
"Okay." I could just about hobble that far.
"Do you want me to show you how it works?" he asked, once we had squeezed into the broom cupboard.
"No, that's okay. I know my way around these things."
"I'll leave you to it then."

I wanted to view the recording of the hours when I-Sweat was closed. Those were the hours that Winky's Moonlight Gym was operational.

I cued the recording to start at midnight the previous day. The display was split into four; each mini-screen showed a different area of the gym. It was deserted, so I fast-forwarded the recording, keeping an eye open for any sign of feline activity, but there was nothing. The first time any movement was picked up by the camera was when Brent came through the doors at just before 8am.

How could that possibly be? It didn't make any sense. Winky was still selling subscriptions, and yet there was no sign that his customers were using the gym overnight. I knew I must have missed something, so I reset the recording, and began to watch it again. This time, though, I didn't fast-forward it. Instead, I watched it in real time.

It made for tedious viewing, and I was just about to give up when I spotted something. A small, white moth landed on the rowing machine closest to the window. I fast-forwarded an hour, and checked again. The moth hadn't moved. Another hour, and the moth was still in the same place. I continued to fast-forward until, at 5am, the moth disappeared. It didn't fly away; it just disappeared.

Eureka!

Winky was on the sofa, fast asleep.
"Okay. How did you do it?" I nudged him.
"Do you mind? I was having an incredible dream."
"Tired from working all night in the Moonlight Gym?"
"Don't you have any work to do? Oh, sorry. Stupid question. Of course you don't."
"What did you do to the CCTV system in I-Sweat?"
"I don't know what you're talking about."
"Don't give me that. I've just been watching the recording. It freezes for several hours overnight."
"They must have bought some cheap kit."
"I know you're behind it. That's why you weren't worried when I told you that they were having the system installed. You might as well tell me how you did it."
"If you must know, I gave Tibby The Hack a free membership. He sorted it for me."
"I take it that Tibby The Hack is a cat?"
"Not just any cat. He can hack anything, anywhere. I suppose this means you're going to grass me up, and get my gym shut down?"
"Not necessarily. There might be a way that you can keep the gym open."
"Go on. I'm listening."
"I could use someone with Tibby's skill-set. If you can persuade him to make his services available to me whenever I need them, then I needn't tell the I-Sweat boys what I know."
"You're even more corrupt than I am."
"Do we have a deal?"
"Okay. Deal."

***

I'd managed to trace Conrad Landers' solicitor. The convicted murderer had already had several appeals rejected, but according to his solicitor, he was busy working on another one. I wanted to speak to Landers if only to rule out any connection between Patty Lake's murder and Angie Potts' disappearance. His solicitor had promised to ask Landers if he would request a visitor's pass for me. Failing that, he was going to see if he could get Landers to speak to me on the phone.

In the meantime, I wanted to meet Sophie Brownling's husband, Lionel. I'd called ahead, and Sophie had confirmed they would both be at home. She met me at the door to their bungalow.

"Lionel is in the lounge," she said, in a hushed voice. "He wasn't very keen on doing this."

"Oh? Why?"

"He doesn't like to see me upset."

"Okay. I'll try to keep it brief."

She led the way into the lounge where her husband, a stocky man with a weather-worn face, was seated on the sofa.

"Jill Gooder. Thanks for seeing me, Mr Brownling."

"Sophie seems to think it might help, but I can't imagine how."

"I've read all of the press clippings that your wife left with me, and I've also checked the newspaper archives at the library, but what I'd really like to know is what both of you think happened to Angie."

"Why are you asking us?" Lionel snapped. "Isn't that

what we're paying you to find out?"

"Lionel!" Sophie scolded her husband. "You promised."

"Sorry." He didn't look it.

"I think someone must have grabbed her off the street," Sophie said. "I don't believe that Angie would have got into a car with a stranger. She was too sensible for that."

"She had been drinking," I said.

"Angie never got so drunk that she didn't know what she was doing."

"What about you, Mr Brownling? What do you think happened?"

"I don't know. How could I?"

"How did you get on with Angie?"

"Okay." He shrugged.

"I imagine that the relationship between stepfather and stepdaughter can be difficult at times."

"What are you implying?"

"She isn't implying anything, Lionel." Sophie put her hand on her husband's arm.

"It sounds like it to me. Angie and I got on just fine. She wasn't as close to me as she was to her mother, but then you wouldn't expect her to be."

"Had there been any particular arguments just before her disappearance?"

"This is beginning to sound like an interrogation." His face flushed. "I had nothing to do with Angie's disappearance, and I don't appreciate the insinuation."

"I'm sorry if that's how it came across, but if I'm going to help, I need to find out as much as I can about the family dynamic."

"What good will that do?" he said. "I told Sophie this was a waste of time and money."

"While I was looking through the archives at the library, I came across an article about a young woman, Patty Lake, who was murdered nine months after Angie disappeared. There was some suggestion that the person who killed her might also have been responsible for Angie's abduction."

"That's it! I've had enough of this." Lionel stood up.

"Please, Lionel." Sophie reached for his hand, but he pulled away.

"You're wasting our time, Ms Gooder. The police dismissed the possibility of any connection between the two cases almost twenty years ago. I've had enough." He left the room, and slammed the door shut behind him.

"Sorry about that," Sophie said. "He means well, but he has a temper. He thinks I'd be happier if I could let all of this go, but how can I?"

"Do you remember the Patty Lake case?"

"Of course. The police came to see us when she first went missing. They must have thought there might be some connection at first, but then Patty's body was found, and we didn't hear any more from them. The next thing we knew, that young man had been charged with her murder. I asked the police if he might have been responsible for Angie's disappearance too, but they were adamant that he wasn't."

"Okay. I'm sorry to have upset your husband."

"He'll be alright. Have you made any progress at all?"

"Not yet, but it's early days. I'd like to speak to the other three women who went out with Angie that night. Do you have their details?"

"I can give you their names, and the last addresses I have for them."

"That will do. I should be able to track them down from

there."

***

On my way back to the car, I checked my phone. I had two text messages. The first was from Jack; he had to work late and so wouldn't be home for dinner. That was just dandy because it should have been his turn to cook. The second message was from Amber. She wanted to remind me about the book signing on Friday. I really wasn't very keen to go, but I felt I should support the twins, so I sent a reply saying I'd be there.

Just then, a woman came down the road, pushing a pram. She was wearing an ankle length blue dress, and a headscarf. There was something very familiar about her.

"Daze?"

"Jill? What brings you to this neck of the woods?"

"I'm working on a missing person case. More to the point, what's with the dress and the pram?"

"Undercover again."

"The dress suits you."

"Don't you start. I've taken enough ribbing from the guys back at HQ."

"Are you working solo today?"

"I wish."

"Hi, Jill." Blaze spat out the dummy, and sat up in the pram.

"Crikey! I didn't realise that was you. It must be a tight fit in there?"

"Tell me about it. I don't know why Daze couldn't have used a doll."

"Because." Daze engaged her 'headmistress' voice.

"This is a two-man job. Plus, I wanted to see you in a pram." She laughed.

"See what I have to put up with, Jill?" Blaze stuck the dummy back into his mouth.

"Who are you after?" I asked.

"We've had reports that Roger Rosepetal, a diminutive elf, is posing as a young child to gain access to the nursery school."

"Why would he do that?"

"Roger is an expert pickpocket. He steals from the parents when they come to pick up their kids. No one expects a young child to be rifling through their pockets and bags."

"He sounds like a nasty piece of work."

"He really is, but he's in for a shock later."

"I bet. Hey, Daze, have you heard of someone called Tammy Winestock?"

"Of course. She's a celebrity chef back in Candlefield. She hit the big time a couple of years ago. What with her TV appearances and books, she must be making a fortune."

"Apparently, she's doing a book signing at Cuppy C on Friday."

"That can't be right."

"According to the twins, it is."

"She's an A-list celebrity. Why would she go to Cuppy C? Are you sure the twins aren't just pulling your leg?"

"I don't think so. They're adamant that it's going to happen."

"If that's right, then kudos to them. Anyway, we'd better get going. We have an appointment with an elf."

"Good luck, Daze." I leaned over the pram. "Oh, and

Blaze—"

"Yeah?" He sat up.

"Goo, goo, goo."

Daze and I dissolved into laughter; Blaze was most definitely not amused.

Chapter 9

Something just didn't ring true about the book signing that the twins had organised. If Tammy Winestock was as big a deal as Daze had suggested, why would she waste her time doing a book signing at Cuppy C? The twins were convinced that it was going to happen, but I had serious doubts.

If I'd had any sense, I would have kept my nose out, but as we've already established, common-sense and I were not even on speaking terms.

I magicked myself over to Candlefield library. I was going to brave the dusty basement where copies of The Candle newspaper were archived. If only the other members of the Combined Sup Council had got their collective heads out of their collective backsides, and agreed to introduce the internet to the sup world, my life would have been so much easier.

Two hours later, covered in dust, I re-emerged. I'd flicked through every copy of The Candle for the last nine months, and had found details of five other book signings that Tammy Winestock had held. They'd all taken place in large, prestigious venues that typically held several hundred people. That seemed to correspond with what Daze had told me, and made it even less likely that the celebrity chef/author would agree to make an appearance in Cuppy C. The most recent book signing that she'd held was at Candlefield Country Club—an upmarket establishment that was located out towards the Black Mountains. That had taken place less than a week before, and according to the article in The Candle, it had attracted a crowd of several hundred eager fans.

"Are you a member?" The wizard doorman at Candlefield Country Club looked down his nose at me.

"No."

"Members only."

"I don't actually want to use the club's facilities. I'd just like to speak to whoever is responsible for booking guest speakers: authors, that sort of thing."

"That's Adrian Knutsmore. You can write to him at this address."

"Is he here now? I'd really like to speak to him today."

"He's a busy man. Who are you, anyway?"

"My name is Jill Gooder. I'm—"

"*The* Jill Gooder? Why didn't you say so?" He stepped aside. "Do come in, Ms Gooder. Take a seat over there, please. I'll see if Adrian is free. Would you care for a drink?"

"No, I'm okay, thanks."

He hurried off, leaving me to reflect that my fame, such as it was, did come in handy sometimes.

A few minutes later, the doorman reappeared. He was struggling to keep pace with a short, older wizard who was headed my way.

"Ms Gooder. This is indeed an honour. I'm Adrian Knutsmore, social secretary."

"Nice to meet you." I shook his hand; he had a strong grip for such a small man.

"To what do we owe this honour? Are you thinking of joining the club? The waiting list is currently over six months, but for you, I'm sure I could pull a few strings."

"That's very kind, but I'm actually here for some

information about a book signing you hosted last week."

"Tammy Winestock?"

"Yes. How did it go?"

"It was a roaring success. We used the main hall, which is very large, but there was barely enough room to accommodate everyone. She's a big draw."

"So I understand. Could I ask how you came to host the event?"

"It wasn't easy to organise. It took me the best part of three months just to get hold of her agent. And when I finally did, he took a lot of persuading. It cost a small fortune, too. Still, she's in such demand, it's hardly surprising."

"Just so I've got this straight. You approached them? They didn't contact you?"

"That's right. Why do you ask?"

"No reason. Thank you very much, Mr Knutsmore. You've been a great help." I turned to leave.

"Are you sure I can't interest you in a membership, Ms Gooder?"

"Not just now, but thanks, anyway."

***

Amber and Pearl were both behind the counter in Cuppy C.

"Hi, girls. Have you ordered the fish tank yet?"

"No. We're going to wait until after the book signing on Friday." Amber was wearing an unusual shade of green lipstick.

"I actually popped in to talk to you about the book signing."

"You're still coming, aren't you, Jill?" Pearl said.

"Yes—err—well, that's just it. I'm worried there might be something amiss about this book signing."

"You worry too much, Jill," Amber said.

"Yeah." Pearl nodded. "You should be more laid back. Like us."

"You might be right, but I've done some research into Tammy Winestock, and it appears that she only ever does book signings at large, prestigious venues."

"Which is why this is such a coup for us," Amber said.

"I've just been to Candlefield Country Club."

"Ooh, la-di-da." Pearl mocked. "Aren't we the posh one?"

"Should we start calling you: your ladyship?" Amber laughed.

"I'm not a member there. I just went to talk to the man who books their guest speakers."

"Are you thinking of giving a talk? Blueberry muffins through the ages?"

They both laughed.

"The club hosted a book signing for Tammy Winestock last week. There were hundreds there—they almost had to turn people away."

"That's great," Amber said. "Think of how much money we'll take over the counter."

"The man who booked Tammy told me that it had taken him three months just to get hold of her agent, and even then, it took some persuasion to get him to agree. They even had to pay her an appearance fee."

"More fool them," Pearl said. "It isn't costing us a penny."

"That's just my point. Don't you think this smells fishy?

Why would her agent contact you, and offer to do this for free? Something isn't right."

"You're forgetting one important thing, Jill," Pearl said.

"What's that?"

"We're the ones who spoke to him. We know what he said, and Tammy will be here on Friday, so you'd better make sure you're early, otherwise you might not get in."

"Don't you think it might at least be worth double-checking?"

"No need. We know what was agreed."

Oh well. No one could say I hadn't tried.

***

Jack was obviously pretending to work late, just to get out of making dinner. That left me with three options. Option one: Make dinner for myself—nah, didn't feel like doing that. Option two: Order dinner in—appealing, but I was spending way too much on takeouts. Or option three.

"Kathy, it's me."

"Hey. You just caught me. I just got back from collecting the kids from school."

"No rest for the wicked. I imagine you've got to make dinner now, too?"

"Of course. It isn't going to make itself."

"Having anything nice?"

"I'm doing a roast. Pete enjoys a midweek roast."

"Hmm, sounds delicious. I'm eating alone tonight. Jack's got to work late."

"Hold on." She laughed. "Are you angling for an invite?"

"What? No, of course not."

"So, why did you call?"

"Err—why did I call? Err—to ask—err—to ask if you found out what all the banging was downstairs at Ever."

"You're such a liar. Would you like to come over for dinner?"

"Okay, but only if you insist."

"You can help Pete to do the washing up. And in answer to your question, no, I still don't have any idea what your grandmother is up to down there, but all the banging has stopped, and the workmen seemed to have finished."

"I'll come over now, then."

"See you shortly."

Yes! Result! Except for the washing up part, but I might be able to sweet-talk Peter into doing that by himself.

What? Who are you calling devious?

"Auntie Jill, I've entered a fishing competition." Mikey was on me as soon as I stepped in the door.

"Let Auntie Jill get inside first, Mikey." Kathy appeared from the kitchen.

"That sounds exciting," I lied. "When is it?"

"On Sunday. Will you come to watch me?"

"Sunday? Err—I might be doing—"

"Of course she'll come, Mikey." Kathy got in first. "She's family. That's why she felt she could invite herself over for dinner today, isn't it, Auntie Jill?"

Touché.

"Thanks, Auntie Jill!" Mikey went charging off upstairs.

"He's really into the fishing now, then?" I said.

"Oh yes. He talks about nothing else. Still, I'm not complaining. I'll take fishing over the drumming every day of the week. Pete enters this competition every year, and Mikey said he wanted to take part too."

"What chance will he stand against all the adults?"

"He won't be competing against them. There are separate competitions for different age groups."

"Isn't it an expensive hobby? All that tackle?"

"It is, but we've sold the drum kit. That paid for most of the stuff he needed. You should get Jack to come on Sunday, too."

"Don't worry. If I have to suffer—err—I mean, if I have to *be there*—then he's definitely coming too. It will be payback for the charity sports competition."

"What charity sports competition?"

"Didn't I tell you? He's roped me into some kind of sports day at his work: sack races, egg and spoon, that kind of thing."

"Oh dear. You were always pretty useless at that stuff when we were at school."

"That's not how I remember it."

"That's because you have a selective memory. Don't you remember when you tripped over the sack, and fell into the Mayor? He spilled his lemonade all over his robe."

"You're making this up."

"Trust me, I couldn't make this stuff up."

"Where's Lizzie?"

"In her bedroom."

"Is she okay? She usually comes to greet me."

"She's been a little quiet for a couple of days. Why don't you go say hello to her?"

Lizzie was on her bed, surrounded by a sea of

frankensteinesque beanies.

"Hi, Lizzie."

"Hello, Auntie Jill." She barely managed a smile.

"Is everything okay? You usually come down to say hello to me."

"Sorry. I'm just sad today."

I sat down on the bed, doing my best not to touch any of the monster beanies. "Why are you sad?"

"Caroline has gone."

"Gone where?"

"I don't know. She didn't tell me. When I went to school on Monday, she wasn't there, and I haven't seen her since."

"Why didn't you tell your mummy that you were feeling sad?"

"Because she doesn't believe that Caroline is real. When I talk about ghosts, she laughs and tells me not to be silly."

"You mustn't blame your mummy for that. Not everyone can see ghosts."

"Why can I?"

"Because you're special."

"Are you and Madeline special, too?"

"I suppose we are. There's one very important thing about having this special power that you have to remember: you mustn't tell other people."

"Why not?"

"It might make them sad because they aren't special too."

"What do you think has happened to Caroline, Auntie Jill?"

"I don't know. Maybe she went away on holiday?"

"Do ghosts go on holiday?"

"Sure. Ghosts do most of the same things we do."

"When do you think she'll come back?"

"I don't know. It will depend where she's gone. I'm sure she'll turn up again in a few days. In the meantime, you have to cheer up because your mummy will worry about you."

"I'm okay now I know that Caroline is going to come back." Lizzie jumped off the bed, and skipped out of the bedroom.

She would be devastated if her BFF didn't come back soon, but at least I'd bought a little time to find out what had really happened to Caroline.

"How did you manage that?" Kathy said.

I shrugged. "I just talked to her about her beanies, and she seemed to cheer up."

"You obviously have a knack with kids. The sooner you have some of your own, the better."

"Don't hold your breath."

It has to be said, Kathy makes a mean roast dinner.

"That was delicious, Kathy," I said after I'd finished.

"It's nice to be appreciated for once."

"Hey." Peter objected. "That's a bit harsh. I'm always telling you how much I enjoy your dinners."

"You should take a leaf out of Jack's book, Pete," she said. "He cooks dinner every night."

"No, he doesn't. We take turns."

"I've seen your idea of taking turns. When we were kids, we were supposed to take turns taking out the trash."

"And we did."

She laughed. "The scary thing is that you probably

believe that."

"It's true."

"If you remember, Mum liked us to do it at eight o' clock in the morning, before we went to school."

"I remember."

"And do you remember how you always did a vanishing act just before eight o'clock every day?"

"She's making this stuff up, Peter."

"I bet Jack would have no trouble believing me." Kathy grinned.

"Anyway, how's business, Peter," I asked.

"Going from strength to strength. In fact, I was going to ask you if you'd get Megan to give me a call."

"Oh? Why?"

"I'm getting to the point where I'm going to have to turn work away. I thought I might refer some of the smaller jobs, which I can't handle, to her. After all, I feel like I owe her for the Washbridge House contract."

"I'll tell her. I'm sure she'll be thrilled. It sounds like she's already building up quite a clientele of her own."

"Great. Ask her to give me a call, would you?"

"Sure. When I was talking to her the other day, she mentioned garden gnomes."

Peter grinned. "They're the bane of my life."

"You too? She said that she gets a lot of requests for them."

"They're very popular."

"And profitable, according to Megan. She reckons she's found a cheap source."

"I had someone call me the other day, offering gnomes at ludicrously low prices, but it all sounded rather dodgy. When I asked about a catalogue, he said he didn't have one; he didn't even know what inventory he had. I told him I wasn't interested—it all sounded a bit too good to be true. Tell her to be careful."

"I will."

"Don't forget to come and watch me on Sunday, Auntie Jill," Mikey shouted, as I was leaving.

"Don't worry, Mikey," Kathy said. "I've just sent a text to Uncle Jack. Just in case Auntie Jill should forget."

"You're so trusting, Kathy."

And before you ask, yes, I did do the washing up, but only because Peter wasn't buying any of my nonsense excuses.

Chapter 10

Jack was hovering over the pan, waiting for the egg to boil.

"Is that all you're having for breakfast? A boiled egg?"

"I had my breakfast earlier while you were still in the land of nod."

"What's with the egg, then?"

"I'm going to get in some practice."

"For what?"

"The egg and spoon race, of course." He scooped the egg out of the pan.

"Please tell me you're joking."

"Why would I be joking? I have to give myself the best possible chance of winning."

"Didn't you say this is supposed to be a fun day?"

"It is, but that's no reason not to take it seriously."

Huh?

He started for the back door. "Why don't you come out after you've finished your breakfast? You can practise too."

"I'd like to, but there's a reason why I can't."

"What's that?"

"I'm not totally insane."

"Okay, but don't blame me if you drop your egg on Saturday."

I watched him through the kitchen window, as he ran up and down the garden, egg and spoon in hand. I considered videoing him, but if I showed it to anyone, chances are they would think I was the crazy one. I did live with this man, after all.

Twenty-minutes later, red-faced, he came back into the house.

"I've mastered it," he said, proudly.

"That's great."

"Are you sure you don't want to try?"

"I'm good, thanks."

"Now I just have to figure out how to get my hands on a sack." He cracked open the egg.

"Are you going to eat that now?"

"Why not? It seems a shame to let it go to waste. It's promising to be a great weekend what with the charity sports competition and the fishing competition."

"We're not actually going to the fishing thing, are we?"

"You promised Mikey."

"I know, but it will be deadly dull. I could always send word that I have to work on a case."

"We're both going. I gave Kathy my word. Which reminds me, I hear you managed to get her to make dinner for you last night."

"I hadn't planned to, but she begged me to go over there. I could hardly say no, could I?"

"That's not quite the way Kathy told it."

Jack left for work before I did. As soon as I stepped out of the door, I heard the sound of Mr Hosey's train, chugging down the road. When he pulled up in front of my house, he didn't look happy.

But Bessie certainly did.

"I like what you did with Bessie," I said, as he stepped down from the engine.

"*I* didn't do it. And, I most certainly *don't* like it!"

Oh dear. Someone had drawn a big smiley face on the

front of the engine.

"Who did it, then?"

"I found her like that this morning, and I have a pretty good idea who was behind it." He glared across the road at Mr Kilbride's house. "You're a detective, aren't you?"

"I'm a private investigator."

"Can you find out if he did it?"

"I'd like to help, Mr Hosey, but I have a strict policy of not taking on cases for neighbours. It can lead to bad feeling."

Just then, I spotted Megan coming out of her door—that was just the excuse I needed to extricate myself from Hosey.

"Megan, hi. I was hoping I'd see you. Sorry, Mr Hosey, there's something I need to talk to Megan about."

He huffed and puffed, and made his way back to Bessie.

"What did you want, Jill?" Megan said.

"Nothing, actually. I was just trying to get away from Mr Hosey."

"Oh, right. I like what he's done to his train."

"He didn't do it. It was sabotage, apparently, and he suspects Mr Kilbride."

"The guy with the bagpipes?"

"Yeah. There's bad blood between them."

"I had no idea there was so much intrigue on the street."

"Trust me, you don't know the half of it. Come to think of it, I do have something to tell you, and I think you're going to be pleased."

"Oh?"

Peter has more work on than he can cope with; he was thinking of sending some of it your way, if you're interested?"

"Really? That would be fantastic. I'm flattered he would think of me."

"He figures he owes you one for what you did on the Washbridge House contract."

"Tell him that I'd be grateful for any work he can put my way."

"Great. I'll let him know. Oh, and one more thing. He said to be wary of that cheap supplier of garden gnomes. Apparently, someone contacted Peter about them too, but he reckons they sound a bit dodgy."

"I wonder if it's the same guy. To be fair, the ones I've bought to-date have been okay."

"Maybe it's not the same person, then. Anyway, just bear it in mind."

"I will. Thanks, Jill. Oh, and by the way, that thing with Ryan is all sorted."

"What thing?"

"You remember. The bottles of red liquid I found in his fridge."

"Oh yeah. What was it?"

"It turns out that it's just an iron supplement."

"I'm glad that's all sorted."

"Yeah. We're good now. In fact, I tried some of it myself. I've been feeling a little tired lately, so I figured an iron supplement might help."

Oh bum! "How was it?"

"Okay, although it did have a weird taste."

***

I was just about to set off for work when my phone

beeped to indicate I had a message. Probably Jack, all excited because he'd found a sack.

It was actually from Grandma.

Drop into Ever on your way into work. I have something to show you.

That familiar feeling of dread resurfaced. Whatever she wanted to show me was unlikely to be good, but what choice did I have?

The shop wasn't actually open when I got there, so I knocked on the door. And then again, and again. I was beginning to think she'd gone out when she appeared, red-faced.

"Haven't you heard of the word patience?" She opened the door to let me in.

"I didn't think you were here."

"I was downstairs; that's why it took me so long."

"Sorry. You said there was something you wanted to show me."

"Indeed, I do. You should feel very honoured to be the first person to see Ever's new offering."

"Which is?"

"Follow me, and you'll see."

She led the way downstairs, into what had been a storage area the last time I'd been down there.

"Can't you switch on the light, Grandma? It's very dark down here."

"Patience. Three, two, one." She threw the light switch.

I was speechless.

"Well? What do you think?"

"It's — err — it looks like — err — is it what I think it is?"

"If you think it's a ballroom, then you'd be right. Isn't it marvellous?"

It really was. The polished wooden dance floor was much bigger than I remembered the basement being. Marble topped tables bordered the dance floor, and above our heads was a huge mirror ball.

"So?" She waltzed onto the dance floor. "Isn't it absolutely stupendous?"

"Yes, but what's it for?"

"Sometimes, I truly despair of you, Jill. What do you think it's for? To raise chickens on?"

"I get that it's for dancing, but what does that have to do with knitting?"

"Precisely nothing, but then you probably think that Ever is a wool shop."

"Isn't it?"

"Ever is a *destination*. It's true that you can buy yarn at Ever, but you can also come here to take afternoon tea, or for a cocktail on the sun terrace. And now, you can come here to dance too. What could be better?"

Just when I thought Grandma couldn't surprise me ever again, she managed to do it.

"I'm very impressed. Have you shown it to Kathy?"

"Not yet. I wanted to show my darling granddaughter first."

"I'm honoured." But very suspicious.

"It's not all good news, though." She sighed.

I knew it. Here we go.

"I've discovered that YarnStormers have taken that vacant building just up the road. I had hoped that you would have come up with some info on them by now."

"I tried, but I drew a blank."

"And people actually pay you to do this stuff, do they?"

As soon as I was outside the shop, I called Kathy.

"Hey, it's me."

"No, you can't back out of coming to the fishing competition. You promised Mikey."

"I'm not calling about that. Jack wouldn't let me back out even if I wanted to. I'm calling because I know what Grandma has been up to in the basement at Ever."

"What?"

"She's got a ballroom down there."

"No."

"Yes. I've just seen it; there's even a mirror ball."

"How come she's shown you, but I'm still in the dark?"

"Because I'm her favourite granddaughter."

"Why a dance floor?"

"Because, and I quote, 'Ever is not just a wool shop, it's a *destination*'."

"What a complete load of —"

"I know, but that's what she reckons. Anyway, you'll be able to see it for yourself when you go in later."

"It's my day off today."

"Tomorrow, then. Anyway, I have to go, but I thought you'd like to know."

"Thanks, Jill."

I'd only gone a few yards when I bumped into Norman, who presumably was on his way to Top Of The World.

"Morning, Norman."

Cue compulsory pause until the words had registered.

"Oh? Morning, err — ?"

"Jill."

"Jill, that's it. Was it you who told me about WashBets?"

"I did indeed. Did you find time to drop in there?"

"Yeah. I went in a few days ago."

"Did you place a bet?"

"No, but I got talking to this really nice woman."

"Her name wouldn't be Tonya, would it?"

"Yeah. How did you know?"

"Lucky guess."

"We really hit it off."

No surprises there. Kindred spirits, if ever I'd seen them.

"Are you going to take her out?"

"Yeah. The trouble is, I can't remember where I said I'd meet her. Or when."

Oh boy!

When I walked into the office, Jules was on her phone.

"It's not my fault. What do you expect me to do about it? Please yourself." She stabbed the screen with her finger, to end the call. "Sorry about that, Jill. Gilbert is doing my head in."

"What's he done now?"

"He's cheesed off because he can't get hold of tickets for ToppersCon. He keeps moaning to me about it. I don't know what he expects *me* to do."

"Are you telling me that stupid thing is sold out?"

"Unbelievable, isn't it? Who would have thought there would be so many idiots interested in bottle tops?" She picked up a note from her desk. "Annabel left this for you."

"Thanks."

It was a reminder that I'd promised to check with Daze to see if Mrs V could take a look around the old sock factory. I'd forgotten all about it.

"Rich, rich, I'm going to be rich." Winky was singing to himself when I went through to my office.
"You sound pleased with life."
"I've had a few brilliant ideas in my time, as you are no doubt aware."
"Modest, as always."
"No sense in false modesty. Of all my brilliant ideas, I think my new app tops the lot. It's going to make me very rich."
"I'm so very pleased for you."
"You should be. You get a five percent cut."
"Twenty, I think you'll find."
"Are you sure about that?"
"Digital recorder. Need I say more?"
"I hate that contraption. Okay. Twenty percent."

I made a call.
"Daze, I'm after a favour."
"Go on."
"Mrs V, my PA, has been doing some research into her family tree, and she's discovered that she's related to the guy who used to own the old sock factory. I happened to mention that I knew someone who lived in the apartments in that building, and Mrs V wondered if there was any way that she could take a look inside. She just wants to get a feel for the history of the place."
"She can come and look around the communal areas, and I can ask Haze if it's okay for her to come into our apartment, if you like?"
"That sounds great. Will you get back to me?"

"Sure. No problem."

Chapter 11

I wanted a closer look at Winky's app, so I used it to search for holiday accommodation in the Washbridge area for the following week. A number of properties were displayed, with filters available to narrow down the search results. After filtering the search to show 'houses only', the number of listings displayed was reduced to just six. Once again, the most notable thing was just how cheap the rental price was. I could not figure out how he was doing it. As I studied the listings in more detail, I recognised one of the properties; it was a house a few doors down from where Kathy lived. When I got the chance, I would ask her if she knew the people who lived there.

***

I had the last known address of Karen Prestwick, one of the women who had been with Angie Potts on the night she disappeared.

Wash Meadows was a picturesque village on the outskirts of Washbridge. There was a pond, complete with ducks, in the centre of the village green. The address I was looking for turned out to be a small thatched cottage that faced onto the green. Given the location, the property had to be worth a fortune.

I knocked using the ornate brass doorknocker.

"Hello?" The woman who answered the door had a vase in one hand, and a duster in the other. "Can I help you?"

"I'm looking for Karen Prestwick. Does she still live

here?"

"Who are you?"

"My name is Jill Gooder. I'm a private investigator."

"What do you want with Karen? I'm her mother."

"I've been hired by Sophie Brownling to investigate the disappearance of her daughter, Angie Potts."

"After all this time? What does she expect to find?"

"She's just hoping to get some kind of closure. Being a mother yourself, I'm sure you can understand that."

"Of course, but I'm not sure how Karen can help."

"I'm hoping to speak to all of those who were with Angie that night. Would you give me Karen's address?"

"It took her a long time to get over this. I don't want you to reopen old wounds."

"It would only be a few questions. Think how you would feel if it was Karen who had gone missing that night."

She was silent for the longest moment, but then she nodded. "Okay. Karen's name isn't Prestwick now; it's Jones. Wait there, and I'll jot down her address and phone number for you."

Not only did Mrs Prestwick give me her daughter's address, but she actually rang ahead and spoke to her. Fortunately, her daughter was more than willing to talk to me, and better still, said that I could go straight over.

Karen's home could not have been a bigger contrast to her mother's. She lived in an apartment block in the centre of Washbridge.

"Jill? Come on in. I'm sorry about the mess."

She wasn't kidding. The place wasn't dirty, but it looked as though someone had tipped it upside down and shaken it. There was stuff everywhere.

"Take a seat, if you can find one."

We were in the living room. I had to move a pile of clothes off the chair in order to sit on it. Karen sat cross-legged on the floor.

"It's a bit different to my mum's place, eh?"

"She has a lovely cottage."

"Lovely, but not lived in. I never felt I could breathe in there. I was too scared of leaving finger marks on something. Let me guess, was she cleaning when you went to see her?"

"How did you know?"

"She always is. It's her hobby."

"I take it your mum told you what this was about?"

"Yeah. I'm really surprised Angie's mum has decided to do something after all this time."

"Is it something you still think about?"

"Of course. I think I always will. It had a profound effect on me that lasted for a very long time. I don't get upset any more, but that doesn't mean I don't still wonder what happened that night."

"What kind of person was Angie?"

"She was the quietest one of the group."

"Had you known her long?"

"Only for a few years. Michelle and I met her at college. Susan Bowles had known Angie since they were kids. She always reckoned that Angie had been much more happy-go-lucky before her father died."

"Did Angie ever talk about her stepfather?"

"Not much, but it was pretty obvious that they didn't get along."

"On the night she disappeared, did you notice anything

unusual about Angie?"

"Nothing. When we all went our separate ways, everything seemed perfectly normal. That's what makes it so weird."

After Karen had answered all of my questions, she was able to give me contact details for the other two women who had been with Angie on the night she'd disappeared. Unless one of them could provide me with more information than Karen Jones had been able to, this case was going nowhere. My only other hope was Conrad Landers, but I still hadn't heard back from him, and there was a good chance I never would.

***

Back at the office, Jules seemed to be much brighter.

"Sorry I was a bit of a grouch earlier, Jill. I shouldn't let Gilbert get to me like that."

"Don't worry about it. Men? Can't live with them; can't shoot them."

"I forgot to mention that Lules asked me to thank you for letting her work here, and for putting her in touch with Megan."

"Has she spoken to Megan yet?"

"Yeah. Lules was on the phone to her for ages last night, and I think she's going to meet up with her. Lules said she was really helpful."

"That's great. Megan has definitely been there, done that, and got the T-shirt."

Once I was in my office, I gave Aunt Lucy a call.

"It's me. I was just wondering if you happen to have a phone number for the Candlefield Special Delivery service? There's something I need to send to CASS."

"I think so. Can you hold on while I try to find it?"

"Sure."

Winky was lying on the sofa, with his head on his paws. I'd assumed he was asleep, but I could see now he was wide awake, and looking very sorry for himself.

"What's up with you, misery chops? Don't tell me the app business is failing."

"Of course it isn't. It's going from strength to strength."

"So why the long face?"

"It's the dinner with Peggy, Carrie and *Tom*, tonight."

"I take it you're not looking forward to it?"

"If it was just me and Peggy, it would be fine. I just can't bear the thought of having to listen to Tom, bragging and putting me down all evening."

"You usually give as good as you get."

"I know, but if I turn on him, it will upset Peggy, so I'm going to have to suck it up. It just doesn't sit well with me."

"I can imagine. Where are you having the meal?"

"In here, obviously."

"Obviously."

"I've ordered in catering."

"I hope you haven't charged that to my—"

"Jill?" Aunt Lucy was back on the line. "Sorry to keep you waiting like that. I knew I had it somewhere. Do you have a pen?"

I scribbled down the phone number.

"Thanks, Aunt Lucy."

"No problem. Oh, and by the way, it seems like I was

worrying over nothing about my new neighbour. I met him yesterday; his name is Glen, he's a wizard, and he seems really nice."

"That's good news. I told you there was nothing to worry about. Will he be living there by himself?"

"No. I haven't met his partner yet, but if she's anything like Glen, I'm sure she'll be very nice too."

"That's great. Bye then."

I called Candlefield Special Delivery, and they promised to have someone around within the hour. That gave me time to draft a quick letter to Desdemona Nightowl. I wanted her permission to visit CASS again so that I could try to find out more about the pendant, the portrait and the initials 'JB'.

I'd promised Harry and Larry that I would investigate the fire at their bakery, in which they had lost their lives. They were convinced it had been arson, and that the man responsible was a certain Stewey Dewey who had run a rival bakery.

A simple internet search led me to numerous articles from local papers, in particular The Bugle. The fire had happened in the early hours of a Monday morning in February. At the time, the only people inside the building had been Harry and Larry. The fire had taken hold quickly, trapping them inside. By the time the fire crew managed to fight their way into the building, both men were already dead. A man had been taken in for questioning, but had been released without charge. That man was Stewey Dewey who ran a rival bakery only a few streets away. The same man that both Harry and

Larry were convinced was responsible for their deaths. Subsequent articles, published some weeks later, stated that the cause of the fire had not been established, but there was no evidence that foul play had been involved.

A visit to Dewey's Bakery was called for.

"Jill." Jules' voice came through the intercom. "I have a man here to see you. He says his name is Puddle."

"Send him in, would you?"

I'd met Laurence Waters, AKA Puddle, when he delivered packages to me from CASS.

"That was remarkably quick, Puddle."

"CSD aims to please. I understand you have a package to be delivered to CASS?"

"Just a letter, actually. How much will it cost?"

"There's no charge to you." He smiled. "I thought you knew. The service is free to all members of the Combined Sup Council."

"I didn't realise. When is it likely to be delivered?"

"If it was anywhere else in Candlefield, I would say within the hour, but it will be at least two hours to CASS. Is that okay?"

"Yes, that's more than quick enough. Thank you very much."

"My pleasure."

In the letter, I'd explained my reasons for wanting to visit CASS. All I could do now was hope that Desdemona Nightowl would give me her permission.

***

H&L Bakery had stood on Washbridge Way. What was

left of the building had long since been demolished, and in its place, there was now a large beauty salon called You Little Beauty. From the articles I'd read, I knew that Dewey's Bakery was just two streets away on Treesmore Road.

Dewey's Bakery had a shopfront from which they sold their range of baked goods. Just looking at the window display was enough to make my mouth water. Their cakes looked to die for, but I was there on business, and I would not allow myself to be distracted.

"Yes, madam?" The man behind the counter was wearing a straw boater, for reasons known only to him.

"Can I get one of those strawberry cupcakes, please?"

What can I tell you? I'm weak, so shoot me.

"That will be two pounds, please."

"Thanks. Is Mr Dewey in today?"

"Stewey?"

"Yeah. I wondered if I could have a quick word."

"You've come to the wrong place."

"Oh? Does he have more than one premises?"

"He's not in the bakery business any longer. He hasn't been for a long time."

"The sign still says Dewey's Bakery."

"The bakery and shop belong to me and my brother. I'm Charlie Grott. When we bought the place, we figured that the Dewey name had a value; it had built up a lot of goodwill. We'd have been crazy to ditch it, and besides, who would want to buy cakes from Grott Bakery?"

"Good point. When did you take over?"

"A few years ago. I assume you heard about the fire at the other bakery?"

"H&L? Yes."

"It was not long after that, that Stewey sold up."

"Do you happen to know where I could find him?"

"Last I heard, he was living out in Smallwash. Do you know it?"

"I should do. I live there. You don't happen to have his address, do you?"

"Sorry, no."

"Never mind. I'll find it. Thanks again for your help." I took a bite of the cupcake. "Mmm. Very nice."

Chapter 12

I was in two minds whether to go back to the office, or to call it a day, but then I got a call from Jules.

"Jill. Sorry to call you on your mobile, but I've had a lady on the phone. She sounds really desperate. She asked if you'd call her straightaway."

"Who was it? Did she say what it was about?"

"She was in such a state, I could barely make out what she was saying. Something about an owl, but I honestly don't know what she was going on about. Sorry."

"That's okay. Did you manage to get her number?"

"Yes, but only because it was showing on Caller ID."

I made a note of the number, and told Jules I'd take care of it. Could it have been Desdemona Nightowl? It seemed unlikely because it was a Washbridge number, and Ms Nightowl didn't seem to be the kind of person who would get so worked up; she always seemed so cool, calm and collected.

"Hello!" The woman shouted so loudly that I had to move the phone a few inches from my ear.

"This is Jill Gooder. I have a message that you wanted me to call you."

"Yes. Thank you. Oh goodness. It's terrible. Please, can you help me?"

"I need you to take a deep breath, and slow down a little."

"Sorry. It's Alfie. You have to help me."

"I'll do my best, but can we start with your name?"

"Sorry. I'm not thinking straight. My name is Brand, Ella Brand. I got your name from Myrtle Turtle. I believe you work with her?"

"I did, but only the once."

"I've known Myrtle for years. She was the first person I thought of, but she's just had a hip operation, and is confined to bed. Myrtle said that you might be able to help."

"I'm snowed under with work at the moment."

"Please Ms Gooder. You're my last hope. You're Alfie's last hope."

"Who is Alfie?"

"He's a barn owl."

"You have an owl?"

"I have lots of them. Other birds too. I run the Washbridge Bird Sanctuary. I've had Alfie for several years. Someone left him on my doorstep with a note that just said his name was Alfie, and asked if I'd look after him. When I went to check on him this morning, he'd gone. Disappeared."

"Has he been stolen?"

"I don't know. I suppose it's possible, but there was no sign of a break-in. Can you help, Ms Gooder? I'm worried about what might happen to Alfie if he's out there all alone."

"Like I said, I am very busy."

"Please, Ms Gooder. I'm begging you."

"Okay. I'll come and take a look, but I'm not making any promises."

"Thank you so much. Myrtle said you were an angel."

I should have been heading home for dinner, but instead I was off on some wild owl chase. I sent Jack a text: *Last minute case cropped up. Won't be in for dinner.*

Moments later, my phone beeped with his reply: *Okay. Take care. See you later. BTW, I've managed to get hold of a sack and am going to practise.*

I'd driven past the entrance to the bird sanctuary twice, before I realised that it was located down a narrow dirt track, off the main road between Washbridge and West Chipping. As I pulled onto the gravel car park, an elderly woman wearing a blue overall and wellingtons, came hurrying over.
"Is it Jill?"
"That's me. You must be Mrs Brand."
"Ella, please. It's what everyone calls me. Did you find us okay?"
"I drove past a couple of times."
"Most people do. The sign blew down three months ago, and we don't have the funds to have it replaced."
To my left was a small cottage, and to my right was the building that quite obviously housed the birds. That much was apparent from the sounds coming from within.
"Is that your cottage?"
"Yes. I've lived here for almost forty years. I started the sanctuary about twenty years ago. I didn't intend to. It started with one kestrel, and it grew into this monster."
"Would you like to show me where Alfie is usually housed?"
"Of course. Follow me."
"Is the sanctuary open to the public?"
"No, dear. We tried that, but it was too upsetting for the birds."
"How do you manage to fund the place?"
"It's a struggle. We do occasionally take some of the

more resilient birds out to the parks in and around Washbridge. That raises some money. Plus, we have our regular donors."

Inside the building, there were dozens of cages housing all manner of birds, some of which I could identify, others I'd never seen before. At the other end of the building was an open door, and beyond that a courtyard, which had not been visible from the car park. There were even more cages and birds out there.

"This is where Alfie lives." Ella pointed to a large empty cage.

"Was the door open when you discovered he'd gone?"

"No. It was closed."

"So whoever took him must have stopped to close the cage door before making their escape? Doesn't that strike you as odd?"

"I suppose so. I hadn't really considered it."

"Was Alfie the only bird taken?"

"Yes, thank goodness."

"Is he particularly rare or valuable?"

"Alfie?" She laughed a hollow laugh. "He's a senior citizen. I love him to bits, but he has no real value to anyone else. Do you think you'll be able to find him, Ms Gooder?"

"I have to be honest. Right now, it isn't looking very promising."

Her face fell, and she looked close to tears.

"Why don't you let me take a look around to see if I spot anything that might help."

"Alright, dear. I'll go and have a cup of camomile tea to soothe my nerves. Can I get you a drink?"

"No. I'm okay, thanks."

I honestly didn't know where to start. I should have told Ella Brand that it was a hopeless case, and that I couldn't help, but I wasn't sure she was up to hearing that just yet. Hopefully, the camomile tea would calm her down a little, and I'd be able to break the bad news later.

"Hey! Witchy!"

The voice made me jump. "Who said that?"

"Over here. Two cages down."

I walked cautiously towards the voice.

"Hello?"

"Over here."

"Was that you?" I said to the small owl.

"Who did you think it was? Turn around, would you?"

"Sorry?"

"Turn to face the other way."

I did as he said.

"Okay. You can turn back again now."

Instead of an owl, there was now a man crouched inside the large cage. He was naked except for a sack he had tied around his waist.

"You're a shifter!"

"No flies on you, are there? I can see why the old biddy called you in. I'm Eric, by the way."

"Nice to make your acquaintance, Eric. Do you know what happened to Alfie, the barn owl?"

"He's a shifter too."

"Oh?"

"It's a cushy number we've got here. The old biddy takes really good care of us, and we can sneak out into the city occasionally."

"Is that where he is?"

"No. He went back to Candlefield to visit his sister. He goes there once a month, but he's always back before morning."

"Do you know what happened to him?"

"No idea. He's never done this before. I'm a bit worried, to tell you the truth."

"Do you have his address in Candlefield?"

"Yeah. He stays at his sister's house when he's over there."

"If you let me have it, I'll go over there tomorrow to see if they have any news on him."

Ella Brand returned a few minutes later.

"What do you think, young lady? Have I lost him for good?"

"I don't know, Ella. Why don't you leave it with me for a day or so, and I'll see what I can find out?"

"Okay, Jill. If Myrtle says you're the real deal, that's good enough for me. I know you'll do your best to bring my Alfie home."

***

I had to drive back through Washbridge on my way home, so I called in at the office in case Jules had left me any messages.

As soon as I walked in, I could hear noises coming from my office. I was just about to charge in there when I remembered that Winky and Peggy were entertaining their two friends.

There were no messages on Jules' desk, so I could have turned around and left, but I didn't. Instead, I climbed onto a chair so I could see down into my office.

What? Don't give me that. You would have done the same thing.

The four of them were seated at the table. Winky looked very smart in his little suit, but Tom had gone the whole hog, and was wearing an evening suit, which must have cost an arm and a leg. It didn't take long for me to understand why Winky disliked Tom so much. That cat was a real piece of work.

"*I got a first in history. What about you, Winky old man? What's your degree?*"

"*Rowing is my game. Got a blue, don't you know. What about you, Winky?*"

"*I really must give you the name of my caterers, Winky. They would put this lot to shame.*"

And on and on it went.

Although I would never admit it to him, Winky had one of the sharpest minds of anyone I knew: human or animal. He could have run rings around that stuck-up little prat, but he didn't. Instead, he took one blow after another until I could bear to listen no longer. If I'd stayed, I would have charged in there, all guns blazing, and told Tom exactly what I thought of him.

***

I knew that Jack would already have had his dinner by the time I got in, so I called at The Corner Shop on my way home. I couldn't face the prospect of cooking dinner for myself, so I intended to get a ready meal.

There was no sign of Jack Corner, but Missy Muffet was behind the counter, standing on a box as usual. She was tucking into something which smelled quite revolting.

"Sorry about this," she said. "Mr Corner asked me to work late, so I'm having to grab a snack on the go."

"No problem. I've had to work late too." I sniffed the air. "What is that you're eating?"

"This? It's curds."

"And whey?"

"Ooh, no!" She screwed up her nose. "That stuff is gross."

"I'll just take this." I put the Pot Noodle on the counter.

"Is that all you want?"

"Yeah. I just need something quick and easy."

"Mr Corner has asked me to tell every customer about his new line."

"What's he got this time? Rubik's Cubes? Space Hoppers?"

"Buckets."

"Sorry?"

"Over there." She pointed down the next aisle.

I shuffled to my left, and took a look. At the far end of the shop was a mountainous display of buckets, in all colours and sizes.

"I've never seen so many buckets."

"He bought a job lot. Can I interest you in one?"

"No, thanks. I'm okay bucket-wise at the moment."

"Will you at least take one of these. It's a list of all the different sizes and colours. It took Mr Corner hours to complete it."

"Okay, then." I turned to leave, but then hesitated. "No thought for the day?"

"Sorry. Mr Corner did tell me what it was, but I've forgotten. You won't tell him, will you?"

"Your secret is safe with me."

When I got home, Jack had his trouser leg rolled up, and was applying a plaster.

"What happened to you?"

"I tripped."

"While you were practising for the sack race?" I grinned.

"I'm glad you find it amusing."

"Sorry. How did it go?"

"Really well, until I fell. I figure I'm in with a good chance of doing the double."

"Good for you."

"What's that in your hand?"

"A Pot Noodle. What does it look like?"

"Not that. The sheet of paper."

"This? It's just a bucket list."

"Aren't you a bit young to be making one of those?"

Chapter 13

Jack had made us both a fry-up for breakfast. What a star!

"I think I've got the sack race nailed." He sounded very pleased with himself.

"That's great."

"I managed to lay my hands on a small sack too if you'd like to practise before you leave for work."

"I'd love to, but I have to see someone before I go to the office."

"I take it you're still busy?"

"Very. I've got a few cases on the go."

"That's what I like to hear." He grinned. "If you keep that up, I'll be able to retire soon, and become a gentleman of leisure."

"Dream on, buddy. I only got together with you because I thought I could become a kept woman."

"You got that badly wrong, didn't you?"

"It's beginning to look that way."

After Jack had left for work, I checked the local phone book. There was only one Dewey listed in the Smallwash area, and he had the initial 'S'. That sounded like my man. Remarkably, he lived only five minutes from my house.

Dewey's house stood out from the rest in the row, but not in a good way. The paintwork was flaking and in desperate need of attention. The lawn was overgrown, and the borders were overrun with weeds. One of the gates was hanging from a single hinge.

I knocked three times on the door, and was about to give up when I heard footsteps inside.

"Yes?" The man who answered the door had long, unkempt hair, and a beard; he looked like he hadn't washed for some considerable time. He was standing awkwardly, with one hand tucked behind his back.

"Mr Dewey?"

"Yes."

"My name is Jill Gooder. I'm a private investigator. Could I ask you a few questions?"

"What about?"

"The H&L bakery."

For the first time, I thought I saw a spark of life in his eyes. "What about it?"

"I understand you were there when it burned down."

"Yes, I was."

"Can you tell me what happened that day?"

"They died. Both of them. I couldn't do anything."

"Did you know the men who died?"

He nodded. "I used to have a bakery, too. We were rivals. We didn't really get on."

"What were you doing there that day?"

"I walked that same route every morning. I saw the flames as soon as I turned onto the street. I tried to get in, but it was impossible."

"Did the police question you?"

"Yes. They thought I'd done it."

"You sold your own bakery not long afterwards. Why was that?"

"I couldn't see any point in carrying on. Harry and Larry worked much harder than I ever did, and look what happened to them. Snuffed out just like that. And anyway, I couldn't work with this." He brought his arm from behind his back. All that remained of his fingers were stubs.

"Did the fire do that?"

He nodded. "Didn't even realise I'd done it until they dragged me into the ambulance. If I could just have got inside the building, I might have been able to save them." He looked me square in the eye. "Why do you want to know all of this, anyway?"

I could hardly tell him that I was working for Harry and Larry, and I couldn't think of any other good answer, so I cast the 'forget' spell, and left.

***

I magicked myself over to Ghost Town. Harry and Larry were both behind the counter in Spooky Wooky.

"Blueberry muffin, Jill?" Harry greeted me with a smile.

"Nothing for me, thanks. I can't stay. Is there any chance I could have a word with you both in private?"

Larry asked one of their assistants to mind the counter while we went into the back.

"I've just been to see Stewey Dewey."

Their expressions changed immediately.

"I hope you told the little scumbag he was going to get what was coming to him," Larry said.

"He didn't do it."

"What?" Harry looked at me in disbelief. "Of course he did it. Surely, you don't believe that lowlife?"

"I am one-hundred percent certain he didn't do it. And what's more, from what I've just seen, Stewey Dewey might as well have died in the fire with you."

"What do you mean?" Larry said.

"He's a broken man. Did you know he sold his bakery

shortly after the fire?"

They both shook their heads.

"The man is living alone, in squalor. I don't know how old he is, but he looks like an old man. It's quite obvious he has lost the will to live. And do you know why? Because he blames himself for not being able to save you. He didn't set the fire, but he did try to get inside to rescue you. The flames beat him back, but not before he'd lost all the fingers off one hand. He still has nightmares about that day; I don't think he'll ever get over it."

"Are you sure about all of this, Jill?" Harry was visibly shaken. "Could he have been putting on some kind of act?"

"That was no act. I'm a good judge of people, and I have no doubt in my mind that he was telling the truth. What I don't understand is why you are both convinced he was responsible for the fire."

"Word got to us that the police had arrested him, and we just assumed he must have done it because the rivalry between us was pretty intense."

"A business rivalry is one thing, but that's a long way from deliberately killing someone. I'm sorry guys, but I think you've got this badly wrong."

***

I wasn't sure if Harry and Larry were convinced or not; they were still in a state of shock when I left them.

While I was in GT, I decided to check in with Constance Bowler. I'd called ahead to confirm she'd be in her office, and could spare me a few minutes.

"Morning, Jill."

"Thanks for seeing me, Constance. I'm actually after a favour."

"If I can help, I will."

"My niece, Lizzie, is exhibiting parahuman powers; she's able to see ghosts."

"How old is she?"

"Only six."

"Is she okay? Has it scared her?"

"She seems fine with it. Lizzie has developed a friendship with one ghost in particular: a little girl named Caroline who normally haunts Lizzie's school. The problem is that Caroline has gone missing. Lizzie hasn't seen her for a few days, and she's a little upset. I told her that Caroline has probably gone on holiday, and that seems to have put her mind at rest for now, but I'm worried about what will happen if the little girl doesn't come back soon."

"How can I help?"

"I wondered if you knew of any way that I could track Caroline down here in GT?"

"You might be in luck. There are special rules governing minors who choose to visit the human world. There's a special register in which they have to be listed, along with signed permission from their parents."

"Is there any way I could get a look at that register? I really need to find Caroline's address."

"I'm afraid that's not possible, but if you can give me the name of the school that Caroline is haunting, I should be able to trace her for you."

"That would be great. Will it take long?"

"I should have the information later today; tomorrow at the latest. I'll give you a call as soon as I have it."

"Thanks, Constance."

"While you're here, Jill, there's something I'd like to show you."

"Sure."

She took a sheet of paper from her top drawer. "One of the biggest problems we are facing is stolen goods that are being taken to the human world. It's easy money for the thieves because they don't even have to worry about fencing the goods here in GT. They simply move them to the human world where they'll never be traced back here. I'm hoping you might help us to put a stop to this."

"What's on the list?"

"Right now, there seems to be a spate of thefts of garden ornaments and gardening equipment. These are the more popular items that are being stolen from properties in GT, and then shipped to the human world."

I ran my eye down the list. One item in particular, caught my attention.

***

I'd just about got used to living in two different worlds, but now that I had a third one to contend with, things could sometimes get confusing. Sometimes, I felt like the lead singer of a rock band who goes on stage and says: 'Hello, Manchester', only to find they are actually in Birmingham.

I'd magicked myself to Washbridge, and from there to Candlefield. I had an owl-shifter to track down, and my first port of call was his sister's house. Appropriately enough, she lived on Aviary Drive.

"Can I help you?" The woman who answered the door

had nails that were so long they resembled talons.

"I'm looking for Alfie."

"Why? Is it about the DVD?"

"Sorry?"

"He took it back three weeks ago."

"I'm not here about a DVD."

"If he owes you money, I haven't got any."

"No, it's nothing like that. I'm working for Ella Brand who runs the Washbridge Bird Sanctuary. She's worried about Alfie."

"Why didn't you say so before? Alfie said someone might come looking for him, but he thought it would be Eric. That's not you, is it?"

"No. My name is Jill Gooder. Do you know where Alfie is?"

"He's in Candlefield Hospital. The stupid idiot went for a bike ride, and fell off. Broke his leg, he did."

"I really do need to have a word with him. Do you know which ward he's in?"

"Dove ward, unless they've moved him. Are you going there now?"

"I thought I might."

"Would you mind taking him a change of underwear? I forgot all about it yesterday."

Dove ward was on the second floor of Candlefield Hospital. Alfie's leg was in plaster, and he was looking very sorry for himself.

"You must be Alfie."

"Who are you?"

"I'm the woman with your clean underwear." I dropped the bag onto his bed. "Your sister sent these."

"Thanks, but I still don't know who you are?"

"My name is Jill Gooder, and I'm working for Ella Brand."

"How is she?"

"She's missing a barn owl, and is extremely worried."

"I knew she would be, but what can I do?" He tapped the plaster cast. "It's my own stupid fault for getting on that bike. I never did have a sense of balance."

"It doesn't look like you'll be back at the bird sanctuary anytime soon."

"The doc said I can get out of here tomorrow, but it'll be weeks before I'm back on my feet. This is a total disaster. I love that gig. I'm well looked after, and I get the chance to raise money for the other 'real' birds that live there."

"Are there many other owl shifters in Candlefield?"

"Quite a few, actually. Most of them are members of the OSA."

"What's that?"

"The Owl Shifter Alliance. I'm the treasurer."

"Who's in charge of the OSA?"

"Graham Clawson is the president. Why?"

"I've had an idea."

***

I'd no sooner arrived back in Washbridge than my phone rang; it wasn't a number I recognised.

"Is that Jill Gooder?"

"Speaking."

"This is Kitty Landers. I'm Conrad's mother. You've been in contact with my son. He says you want to visit him, or talk to him on the phone. He's asked me to find out what it's all about."

"As I said in my note to your son, I'm a private investigator. I'm working for Sophie Brownling. Her daughter went missing several months before the Patty Lake murder."

"I remember. I thought at one time they were going to try to pin that on Conrad too. You know that my son is innocent, I assume?"

"I know he pleaded not guilty, and has had a number of appeals rejected."

"They wanted him to take a plea bargain for a lesser charge, but he refused because he hadn't done anything wrong."

"Sophie Brownling is desperate to find out what happened to her daughter. As a mother, I'm sure you can understand that."

"Of course I can, but I have to tell you, Miss Gooder, that my only interest is in proving my son's innocence, and getting him out of prison. I fail to see how he can help with your enquiry. He was no more involved with that girl's disappearance than he was with the murder."

"It's possible that whoever abducted Angie Potts may also have been responsible for Patty Lake's murder. It's also possible that I may uncover evidence in the course of my enquiry that helps your son, but I do need to speak to him."

"I'm not sure."

"What do you have to lose?"

"I'll talk to him, and see what he says, but I'm not making any promises."

"That's all I can ask."

Chapter 14

What a day! So far, I'd searched for an owl in Candlefield, and a little ghost girl in GT. And, on top of that, I'd had to try to convince Harry and Larry that the bakery fire wasn't arson.

I definitely deserved a coffee.

Did you notice? No mention of muffins? I have such willpower.

"What can I get for you today?" The hipster who was working behind the counter in Coffee Triangle was new.

"Just a caramel latte, please."

"Muffins are on special offer today, if you're interested? Twenty percent off."

"Go on, then. I'll take a blueberry one."

What? You didn't expect me to turn down a special offer, did you?

"Eating in?"

"To-go, please."

"Every coffee bought today earns you one entry in the 'how many marbles in the jar' competition." He pointed to the large jar behind the counter. "Here, just write your name and your guess on this slip of paper."

"Thanks." I'd never been very good at that kind of competition, so I wrote the first number that popped into my head.

As soon as I left Coffee Triangle, I heard music, and if I wasn't mistaken, it was a Viennese waltz.

That's when I saw them.

Half a dozen couples were waltzing up and down the high street. The men were wearing tailcoats; the women

were resplendent in ballgowns. Each of them had a small card pinned to their back, on which was printed:
Ever Ballroom Opens On Monday
At Ever A Wool Moment

Much as it pained me to admit it, Grandma was a marketing genius.

It took me some time to weave my way through the couples who were now dancing a quickstep.

"Jill! Morning!" Betty Longbottom called from across the road.

I popped the rest of the muffin into my mouth, and went over to say hello.

"What's going on over there, Jill?"

I still had a mouthful of muffin, so I grunted, and hoped it sounded like: 'Grandma'.

"Sorry?" Betty obviously didn't speak MuffinGrunt.

I held up a finger to indicate I needed a moment.

"Sorry about that." I'd swallowed the last of the muffin. "It's Grandma. She's opening a ballroom in the basement of Ever A Wool Moment."

"Why would she put a ballroom in a wool shop?"

"Didn't you know? Ever isn't a wool shop. It's a *destination*."

"A what?"

"Don't ask me. That's just some rubbish Grandma came up with. You have to hand it to her, though—she really knows how to generate publicity."

"Talking of publicity." Betty's face suddenly lit up. "Crustacean Monthly are doing a profile on me for their next issue."

"I assume they're a big player in the crustacean world?"

"The biggest."

"You must be delighted."

"I am." Her smile faded a little. "It's just that—I—err"

"What's the problem?"

"When they contacted me about doing the profile, they asked me a number of preliminary questions over the phone. One of the things they asked was if I had a boyfriend, and I said yes."

"Well you do, don't you? I assume you're still seeing Sid?"

"I am, and I think the world of him, but I'm not sure he has the right image for the readers of Crustacean Monthly. He's a bit on the *rough* side. Don't get me wrong; that's one of the things I like about him, but I don't think it's the image I should be projecting for the business."

"What are you going to do?"

"Sid doesn't know about any of this, so I'm thinking of hiring a male escort to act as my boyfriend when the magazine comes to interview me."

"Right. I suppose that could work."

***

When I walked into the office, Mrs V was waltzing around the room with an imaginary partner, and she almost collided with me.

"Careful, Mrs V."

"Sorry, dear. I got a little carried away there. I take it you've heard the good news?"

"What good news?"

"About the new ballroom, of course."

"Oh? *That* good news."

"It's exciting, isn't it?"

"Very."

"I know your grandmother and I have our differences, but I have to give credit where credit is due, this is a masterstroke. There isn't much for the older population of Washbridge to do; most places cater for the younger crowd. I have a feeling this ballroom will be very popular with the senior citizens." She took a deep breath; the dancing had clearly taken it out of her. "I imagine you'll be a regular there, Jill?

Huh? "I'm not a senior citizen."

"I realise that, dear, but I know how much Jack loves to dance."

Oh bum! I hadn't thought of that. I would have to make sure he didn't find out about the ballroom.

"I don't think so. We both have a lot on our plates right now. Incidentally, I heard back from my friend, and we can go over to the sock factory apartments later today if you're still keen to see them?"

"Definitely. Thank you. I'm really excited at the prospect of being in the building where my ancestor once worked. Tobias Fotheringham—such a noble name, don't you think?"

"I guess so. I'll give you a shout later, then."

Winky looked down in the dumps.

"Morning, Winky. How did the dinner go?"

"Don't ask."

"That bad, eh?"

"If I have to spend another evening with Tom, I won't be responsible for my actions."

"He did sound like a bit of a prat."

"How would you know?"

Oh bum! "I—err—I was in the outer office."

"Were you eavesdropping?"

"No, of course not. I just came in to check if Jules had left any messages for me, and I happened to overhear a few things he said. I'm surprised you didn't floor him."

"He thinks he's something special, but he's actually just a—"

"How about some salmon to cheer you up?"

"That's the first sensible thing you've said. This month."

"Cheek."

"Incidentally, my crew have reported back on the surveillance detail."

"Has Lolly's boyfriend been stalking her?"

"No. My guys have tailed him twenty-four seven for the last few days, and he hasn't been anywhere near Molly."

"Lolly."

"Whatever. He hasn't been near her."

"Right. Thanks for that. It doesn't look like she has anything to worry about after all."

"Do you want me to call my chaps off?"

"Have them follow him over the weekend, would you? Just to be sure."

"Okay. Now, where's that salmon? A cat could die of starvation."

***

As Mrs V and I made our way over to the old sock factory apartments, she talked non-stop about Grandma's new ballroom. If Mrs V's enthusiasm was anything to go by, it appeared that Grandma had identified a gap in the market, and stood to make a pretty penny from her new enterprise.

Daze was waiting for us outside the apartment building.

"Daze, this is my PA, Mrs V."

"Pleased to meet you, Mrs V."

"Do call me Annabel. Everyone does."

Huh? Everyone except me, apparently.

"Jill tells me that a relative of yours owned this place when it was the old sock factory?"

"That's right, dear. I suspect it looks a lot different now."

"On the inside, maybe, but from what I hear, most of the original building is pretty much the same. Would you like to take a look inside? I'm afraid I can only show you around the communal areas and my apartment."

Mrs V took a sheet of paper from her bag, unfolded it, and put it up against the wall. "I got this from the library. It's a copy of the old plans of this building, dating back to the time when my relative was alive. It would appear that his office used to be located right there." She pointed to the spot.

Daze studied it carefully. "I'm no expert on this kind of thing, but if I'm right, his office would have been where the third-floor apartments are now. In fact, that appears to be where Charlie lives." Daze turned to me. "You remember Charlie, don't you, Jill?"

"Is that the were—"

"Yes! It's *were* the guy with the cat named Pretty lives." Daze had interrupted me just in time. I'd been about to say: *werewolf*. She turned to Mrs V. "I can't make any promises, Annabel, but Charlie is a nice guy. If you like, we can check if he's in, and if so, ask if you could take a look inside his apartment?"

"Would you, dear? That would be lovely."

Daze led the way to the third floor, and knocked on the door.

"Yes?"

It wasn't Charlie who answered; it was Dorothy. She clearly wasn't pleased to find a rogue retriever on her doorstep.

"Hi, Dorothy." I stepped forward.

"Jill? I didn't see you there."

"Is Charlie in?"

"He's at work."

"Oh, okay. It doesn't matter."

Just then, a young man appeared at Dorothy's side. I recognised him as the wizard who managed the fancy dress shop.

"Hi. I'm Neil. Don't I know you from somewhere?"

"I came into your shop recently to hire a vampire costume."

"Oh, yeah." He grinned. "How did you get on at SupsCon?"

"We won the vampire section."

"That's rather ironic, seeing as how you're a—"

"Neil! This is Mrs V. She's my PA."

"Nice to meet you both." Mrs V stepped forward.

"Likewise," Neil said. "What did you want Charlie for?"

"Actually, the reason we're here is that Mrs V has been researching her family tree. It turns out that one of her relatives used to own the sock factory many years ago. What was his name, Mrs V?"

"Tobias Fotheringham."

"We were going to ask Charlie if we could take a quick look around your apartment because, according to the plans, this is where his office was based."

"Come on in." Neil stepped aside to allow us to enter. As he did, I caught Dorothy shoot him a look. She plainly wasn't thrilled at him inviting a rogue retriever into the apartment. "This is the room you want." He began to walk towards one of the bedrooms.

The three of us followed.

"After you." He held open the door, and Mrs V and Daze stepped inside.

I grabbed Neil's arm, and whispered, "How did you know this room was his office?"

"Socky's ghost still haunts this bedroom."

"Socky?"

"Sorry. That's what we call Tobias. Although I wouldn't recommend you say it to his face."

Neil and I joined Daze and Mrs V inside.

"Isn't this exciting!" Mrs V was taking it all in. "To think my relative once walked this very floor." She shivered. "It's very cold in here, isn't it?"

"The heating is on the blink," Neil said.

He was lying. The reason that the room was so cold was standing over by the window. The male ghost had a wooden leg, and unless I was very much mistaken, he was Tobias Fotheringham, AKA Socky. He didn't look very happy about the intrusion.

Neither Mrs V nor Daze could see the ghost, but Neil and I watched as Socky made his way over to us.

"What's the meaning of this invasion?" Socky addressed Neil.

"Shush!"

"Did you say something, dear?" Mrs V turned to Neil.

"No. I was just sneezing."

"This is not some kind of showroom." Socky complained. "This is my office. Get them out of here now!"

"It's funny," Mrs V said. "It's almost as though I can feel his presence in this room."

"Maybe you'd like to take a look at Daze's apartment now, Mrs V?" I suggested.

She took another look around the room. "I don't think that will be necessary. I've seen all I need to see. I feel as though I've made a connection with the past."

Little did she know that she was only inches away from Socky, who seemed far less enamoured of her.

"Thank you so much for letting me look around," Mrs V said, as we made our way out of the apartment.

"My pleasure." Neil held the door for us. "Call again anytime."

Chapter 15

As we made our way back to the office, Mrs V was still on cloud nine.

"I can't believe I was in the same room that Tobias once stood in. I know you'll think I'm just a crazy old woman, but it almost felt as though he was there with me."

"I don't think you're crazy at all."

"Today has inspired me to trace even more of my ancestors."

"Good for you, Mrs V."

We were only a few streets from the office when I spotted a familiar face down an alley. A familiar feline face, to be precise.

"Mrs V, would you mind going on ahead? I've just remembered something I need to do."

"Another muffin, dear? Think of your waistline."

"No, not a muffin. There's something I need to check. I'll only be a few minutes."

"Okay, but don't forget what I said about your waistline."

Cheek! Anyone would think I did nothing but eat muffins all day.

Once Mrs V was out of sight, I edged my way down the alley. I didn't want to alert my quarry before I'd had a chance to gather the evidence I needed. There were several large waste bins, and I managed to move from one to another without being spotted. When I got as close as I dared, I took out my phone and snapped a few photos.

Gotcha!

***

It occurred to me that if Ella Brand didn't hear from me, she might fly into a blind panic. As I saw it, I had two options. Option one was to tell her the truth:

Your owl is actually a supernatural creature who shifts into owl form. Oh, and by the way, the reason he hasn't come back is that he fell off his bike.

Maybe not.

Option two, and the one I decided to go with, was to try to set her mind at ease for now. That way, I would buy myself time to actually try to sort out the mess.

"Ella, it's Jill Gooder."

"Have you found him, Jill? Have you found Alfie?"

"Not yet, but I think I might be onto something. I won't know for sure until after the weekend, so please don't get your hopes up just yet."

"I'll try not to. Thank you, Jill. I really do appreciate this."

Next, I called Aunt Lucy.

"I'm really sorry to ask, Aunt Lucy, but I wonder if you could do me a small favour?"

"Of course, dear. Anything."

"Would you see if you can find contact details for OSA, the Owl Shifter Alliance. I need to speak to whoever is in charge there as a matter of some urgency."

"No problem."

"Will you be in Cuppy C later for the book signing?"

"I don't have any choice. The twins would never forgive me if I didn't go."

"Okay. I'll see you there later, then."

***

Mrs V was busy updating her family tree, and barely noticed my arrival. Winky was still down in the dumps, but I suspected that was about to change.

"Say thank you, Winky."

"What for?" He looked puzzled.

"For being such a wonderful friend to you."

"Have you been in the wine bar again?"

"I haven't had a single drink."

"Then what are you going on about?"

"There's something on my phone that I think you're going to want to see."

"If you've downloaded some stupid game app, I'm not interested."

"It's not a game. It's photos of your friend, Tom."

"Why would I want to see a photo of him? I'm doing my best to forget his ugly mug."

"I think you'll want to see these." I held up my phone, and began to swipe through the photos, which had captured Tom, flirting with two female cats—neither of whom was Carrie.

"Give me that." He snatched it from my hand. "When did you take these?"

"A few minutes ago—in an alley just down the road."

"Can I have copies?"

"Of course. I can email them to you."

"Why don't you put them into our shared Dropbox. It will be easier."

"Since when did we have a shared Dropbox account?"

"Since I opened one using your business credit card." He handed back the phone. "Tom is soooo dead."

"Haven't you forgotten something?"

"Don't worry. I'm going to email them to Peggy and Carrie in a few minutes. I just need to come up with an appropriate message."

"I was thinking more of a 'thank you'."

"Yeah, of course. Thanks. You did good."

After I'd got over the shock of receiving praise from Winky, I spent some time on the phone, tracking down Susan Bowles and Michelle Wright—the two other women who had been with Angie Potts on the night of her disappearance. They both agreed to meet with me, and I set up separate meetings with them for the following Tuesday.

"Jill." Mrs V appeared in the doorway. "I have a Mr Puddle out here. He has a letter for you, but he won't leave it with me."

"That's fine. Send him in, would you?"

Puddle was smiling as always. "I'm sorry, but I couldn't leave this with your secretary; the rules are very clear on this kind of thing."

"That's okay, Puddle."

"Would you like me to wait for a reply?"

"Yes, please. Take a seat."

"That's a very handsome cat you have there."

Winky's ears pricked up at that. He jumped off the sofa, and onto Puddle's lap.

"Get down, Winky. Puddle doesn't want your hairs all over his uniform."

"He's okay." Puddle began to stroke him. "I have two of my own, but they're not as handsome as this fellow."

Winky would be unbearable after this.

I read the letter from Desdemona Nightowl.

Apparently, it was the last week of term at CASS, and they were busy with exams. She asked if I'd mind delaying my visit until the following week. That wasn't a problem, so I scribbled a quick reply in confirmation. After slipping it into an envelope, I handed it to Puddle.

"Come on, boy. You'll have to get down now." He lifted Winky gently onto the floor.

As soon as Puddle was out of the door, Winky was on my desk. "Did you hear what he said?"

"Can't say I did."

"Handsome, he said."

"Did he?"

"You don't realise just how lucky you are to have me."

"I should do. You tell me often enough."

***

I arrived at Cuppy C much later than I'd planned. So late in fact, that I couldn't get through the door. I'd thought the place had been busy for the Adrenaline Boys, but it was nothing compared to this. The twins certainly had come up trumps this time. I was just about to leave when it occurred to me that I might be able to sneak in the back way, so I walked around the building until I came to the alley, where the drive-thru had been situated for a short and inglorious period of time.

Parked outside the back of Cuppy C, level with the redundant serving hatch, was an old green van that had seen better days. The bodywork was rusty, and two of the tyres were almost bald.

"The drive-thru has closed," I shouted to the scruffy-looking wizard.

"That's okay. I'm not here for food." He opened the back door of the van; it was full of books. "I'm doing a book signing, but I couldn't get through the front door. Do you think I'll be able to pass them through this hatch?"

"What's your name, if you don't mind my asking?"

"Timmy Vinestock."

"Timmy? Vinestock?"

"Yes. Have you heard of me?"

"Sorry. I can't say I have. What's your new book called?"

"A Hundred Things to do with Asparagus."

"Right. Would you like a hand with those books?"

"Yes, please. That's very kind."

Timmy climbed through the hatch, and I passed the books to him.

"Tell me, Timmy. Do you do many book signings?"

"Not many. In fact, hardly any really. Generally, people aren't very interested, but my agent said the twins, who run this place, were very keen."

"I suppose you must get mixed up with Tammy Winestock quite often?"

"Who? Can't say I've ever heard of her."

I suspected that he would have before the day was over.

After I'd passed the last of the books to him, I decided to make myself scarce. I didn't want to be around when the asparagus hit the fan. Back at the front of the shop, I bumped into Aunt Lucy who was with a man I didn't recognise.

"Jill? I guess you couldn't get inside either?"

"Not a chance."

"Pity. I'd have liked to see Tammy Winestock."

"I don't think you're missing much. Trust me on this

one."

"I'm glad I bumped into you, anyway. This is Joseph Feathers. He's the president of OSA. When I mentioned that you wanted a word, he insisted on coming to see you in person."

"I hope you don't mind, Ms Gooder." Joseph stepped forward, and offered his hand. "I'm a big fan. I first saw you in the Levels competition. I knew then that you would go far."

"That's very kind. I wanted a word about one of your members: Alfie, the barn owl."

Joseph nodded. "A little bird told me he'd had an accident."

"That's right. He came off his bike, and broke a leg. He normally lives in a bird sanctuary in Washbridge, but if he's missing for too long, he may not be able to return there."

"How exactly can I help?"

"I imagine you have other barn owl shifters in your group?"

"Oh yes. Several of them."

"I wondered if there was any chance some of them could stand in for Alfie until his leg has mended?"

"I don't see why not. Alfie is one of our most popular members. Why don't I ask around? If enough volunteers come forward, they could share the duties—perhaps one day each."

"That would be fantastic. Thank you very much."

"I'll liaise with your aunt. She can let you know what I manage to sort out."

***

I magicked myself back to Washbridge, picked up the car, and drove home. No doubt I would hear all about the fallout from the Tammy Winestock/Timmy Vinestock incident in due course.

Jack's car was already on the driveway, but before I went inside, I wanted a quick word with Megan. She came to the door wearing a T-shirt emblazoned with a large smiley face.

"Sorry to bother you, Megan."

"Would you like to come in?"

"No, thanks. I just have a quick question for you. Could you give me the contact details for the cheap garden gnome supplier that you mentioned to me?"

"Oh dear." She blushed. "I didn't realise that you and Jack like gnomes. I hope you weren't offended by what I said about them?"

"Not in the least. The gnome isn't for us. It's for—err—my PA, Mrs V."

"Phew. I have a habit of opening my mouth, and putting my foot in it. Just hold on there. I have his business card somewhere."

She disappeared back into the house for no more than a minute.

"There you go."

The card read: *Gnomeing At The Mouth. Proprietor: Tony Tallhats.*

It also included his phone number.

"Thanks, Megan. Mrs V will be delighted."

When I walked into my house, I could hear voices. It was Kathy and Jack.

"What are you doing here?"

"Charming." Kathy rolled her eyes. "How about: *nice to see you, sis?*"

"*Nice to see you.* Now, why are you here?"

"Pete is giving someone a quote for a job, so I asked him to drop me here until he's done. I wanted to give you my big news: I've decided to take the job at YarnStormers."

"Have you told Grandma yet?"

"No. I'll tell her on Monday."

"Can I watch?"

"Watch what?"

"You, telling her that you're leaving."

"I'm sure she'll be okay about it. We're all professionals, after all."

"Yeah." I laughed. "You keep telling yourself that."

"Why didn't you tell me the other big news of the week?" Jack chimed in.

"What big news?"

"About the new ballroom that opens next Monday."

I shot Kathy a look. "You told him?"

"Why not? I know how much Jack loves to dance. You two will have a great time there."

I'd said it before, but I'd say it again: Kathy. Was. So Dead.

Chapter 16

It was Saturday morning, and I should have been looking forward to a leisurely day, but instead the dark shadow of the charity sports competition was hovering over me.

"It's been raining during the night." I was staring out of the kitchen window.

"It was only a little drizzle." Jack was reading his bowling magazine.

"If it's too muddy, maybe they'll call it off."

"I doubt it. A bit of mud never hurt anyone."

"How many events are we taking part in?"

"I'm in the egg and spoon race, the sack race and the tug-of-war."

"What about me?"

"You said you didn't want to overdo it, so I've only put you down for the egg and spoon race. I could still sign you up for some others if you like?"

"No. Just the one will be fine. Does that mean I'll be competing in the same race as you?"

"No. There are separate races for men and women. The only mixed event is the tug-of-war; that's the final event of the day."

"Will Leo Riley be there?"

"I don't know, but I would expect so. Do you think Kathy and Peter will come and watch?"

"Not if they've got any sense. Besides, I imagine Peter will be working."

"I still can't believe you didn't mention that your grandmother was opening a ballroom."

"I meant to, but it totally slipped my mind."

"We should go there on Monday, after work."

"Are you insane? That's opening day. With all the publicity that Grandma has thrown at it, the place will be heaving."

"I suppose you're right. Perhaps it would be best to wait a while until the novelty wears off."

"Yeah." Like a decade or two.

When we stepped out of the door, Jack stopped dead in his tracks; I almost ran into the back of him.

"What's going on over the road?" He was staring at Mr Kilbride's house, which now had what appeared to be a sad face. The upstairs windows formed the eyes, and beneath those, someone had drawn a nose and a sad mouth. "Do you think Mr Kilbride did that?"

"No, but I'm pretty sure I know who did."

"Who?"

"I'll give you a clue. He has a thing about trains."

"Mr Hosey? Why would he have done it?"

"They're having a bit of a dispute. Mr Kilbride did something similar to Bessie."

"Who's Bessie?"

"Mr Hosey's train. The one he drives around the streets."

"How do you know so much about our neighbours?"

"It isn't through choice, believe me."

The charity sports competition was being held on a large green known as Washbridge Meadows. The Washbridge contingency were on the left-hand side of the green, gathered in two groups: men and women. The West Chipping crowd were huddled in two similar groups on the opposite side of the green.

"Gather around." A woman, wearing a tracksuit and running shoes, seemed to be in charge of our group. "For those of you who don't know me, I'm Felicity Anchors. I'm a dog-handler at West Chipping station. If you haven't taken part in this event before, there's something very important that you should keep in mind: This is a *fun* day."

I was relieved to hear her emphasise that point. The way Jack had been going on about it, I'd been worried that people might be taking this way too seriously.

"And we all know the best way to have fun," she continued, "is to crush the opposition. Crush them! Crush them!" She led the chant.

Oh bum!

There were several events before the egg and spoon race, so after Felicity had finished with the pep talk, I found a sheltered spot under a tree, to wait it out.

"Jill? It is Jill, isn't it?" Felicity had found me.

"Yeah. I'm just waiting for the egg and spoon race."

"We've lost a couple of people with flu. Wusses!" She laughed like some kind of mad woman. I was beginning to think I'd rather face her dog than her in a fight. "I'm going to need you to take part in the tug-of-war."

"Won't the rope burn my hands?"

"Sorry?" She glared at me.

"Nothing. Sure. Tug-of-war—no problem."

I wondered if there would be time to nip back to the house to get some gloves, but decided I'd better not. If Felicity saw me sneaking away, there was no telling what she might do.

By the time it came to the men's sack race, the scores were tied. Standing next to one another on the start line were Jack and Leo Riley. I hadn't seen Miley; she'd obviously had the good sense to give this purgatory a miss.

"Come on, Jack!" I yelled.

What? I can be supportive when I try.

The official counted down, and then they were off. The expression on Jack's face was hilarious; never had anyone concentrated so hard on a sack race. There were six contestants in total, but only two of them were really in with a chance. Jack and Leo were several yards in front of the others. Three quarters of the way through, and there was nothing between them. This was going to be really close.

"Come on, Jack! Crush the little toad!"

That attracted a few disapproving looks, but I didn't care.

With only yards to go, it looked like being a draw, but then Leo leaned to one side, and appeared to knock Jack off balance. Jack fell to the floor, and Leo continued over the winning line.

"Hey! Ref!" I yelled. "Did you see that?"

My appeal was in vain because, as far as I could tell, there was no referee. Riley had a huge smile on his face, and was punching the air. Jack had got back on his feet, but ended the race in last place.

I went charging over to him. "Riley tripped you up."

"It was probably an accident."

"What? That was no accident. He deliberately leaned into you."

"Don't make a fuss. It's only a fun day."

"But that little—"

"Jill! It really doesn't matter. It's the women's egg and spoon race next. If you win, that will level us up on points."

No pressure then.

At this point, I should just set the record straight. I hadn't intended to use magic in the egg and spoon race. I'd planned to give it my best shot, and allow the dice to fall as they would. But things had changed. That little weasel had cheated, and what's more he'd nobbled my man.

Yes, you heard right: *my man*.

And let me tell you, no one messes with my man, and gets away with it. To heck with fair play and the Queensberry Rules. The gloves were off.

There were five others lined up alongside me at the starting line, but the poor unsuspecting fools didn't stand a chance because I had cast a spell which effectively glued the egg onto the spoon.

"Three, Two, One, Go!"

I sprinted down the track, paying little heed to the spoon in my hand. I didn't have to worry about it because a hurricane wouldn't have dislodged that egg. Moments later, I crossed the finish line in first place—several yards in front of the pack.

"Well done!" Jack picked me up and spun me around.

When he put me down, someone said, "How is that egg staying on there like that?"

Only then did I realise that I was holding the spoon almost vertically.

"Is it glued on?" someone else shouted, and a crowd began to gather.

"Of course not." I laughed, and quickly reversed the spell, causing the egg to fall to the ground. "See! No glue!"

A few people still looked puzzled, but they had no choice but to let it go.

"It's all down to the tug-of-war now," Jack said. "You have to come and cheer me on."

"I'm in the tug-of-war too. Felicity conscripted me."

"Really? That's great. We'll make a brilliant team. We can't possibly lose."

By the time the two teams were lined up for the final event of the day, all pretence that the competition was just about 'fun' had well and truly been set aside. Everyone was desperate to win, and no one more so than Jack and Leo.

And of course, me.

Even though I was determined that we should prevail, I'd made up my mind that this had to be a clean, fair contest in which the best team would win. It would have been totally unethical of me to use magic in order to give my team an unfair advantage. You can say many things about me, but I have a strong moral compass.

On the rope, I was standing immediately behind Jack. Leo Riley was at the front of his team—his face was taut with determination.

"Three, two, one, go!"

I'd been right about the 'hands' thing; the rope burned my palms as I fought to pull my weight. For a few minutes, it seemed that there was no obvious favourite. The ribbon, which was attached to the centre of the rope, moved no more than a couple of feet in either direction, and then just as quickly, returned to the centre.

"Pull! Riley yelled.

"Pull!" Jack echoed.

My arms were aching, my legs had almost turned to jelly, and my palms were burning, but there was no way I could ease up. But then, suddenly, the woman in front of Jack let go of the rope, and walked away.

"Sorry. I can't do any more." She shook her head.

Her capitulation emboldened the other team who pulled even harder. We were losing the battle; it was only a matter of moments before the game would be up.

It didn't matter. We'd done our best. It was only a game after all.

Stuff that!

I cast the 'power' spell, and immediately things turned around. The other side stood no chance as they were dragged slowly our way.

"Pull!" Riley urged his team on to one last effort, but then lost his footing, and fell face first into the mud.

Moments later, we had won.

"We did it!" Jack gave me a hug, and a big kiss. "We won!"

And so it was that West Chipping won the charity sports competition. You might think that I felt good about that. And you would be so right!

What? Ethical? Smethical. We won, didn't we? And seeing Leo Riley face down in the mud was a bonus.

***

That evening, Jack and I had a few celebratory drinks to toast the win.

"Did you see Riley's face when he fell over?" Jack laughed.

"He's an ugly toad. The mudpack might have improved him."

"I thought we'd blown it when Gillian walked off, but it was as though we suddenly found reserves of hidden strength from somewhere. Did you feel that too?"

"I did. It was a magical feeling."

"At least tomorrow we'll be able to sit back and relax. Watching Mikey's fishing competition shouldn't be too taxing."

If only. It was okay for Jack. He didn't have a sponsored tandem bike ride to get through.

With Grandma.

Chapter 17

"Leave me alone! It's Sunday!" I said when Jack nudged me, and told me to get out of bed.

"It's Mikey's fishing competition."

"What time does it start?"

"Eight."

"Eight o' clock? The fish will still be in bed then."

"Come on. Mikey will be disappointed if we aren't there for the start."

"Couldn't you just take a life-size cardboard cut-out of me, and stand that on the riverbank?"

"Get up!" He started to tickle my feet.

"Stop! Stop! Please stop! I'll get up."

I hated that man.

"What do you want for breakfast?" he asked when I eventually made it downstairs.

"Custard creams, and lots of them."

"You can't have custard creams for breakfast. It isn't healthy."

"Just you watch me." I took out the packet, and put three onto a plate.

"Three?" He looked horrified.

"You're right." I took another one from the pack. "I'm going to need these to get me through the day."

"It's only a fishing competition. All you have to do is watch Mikey."

It wasn't the fishing competition that was bothering me, although I'd have gladly given that a miss if I'd thought I could get away with it. It was the bike ride that I was dreading. My poor hands were still sore after the tug-of-war. How was I meant to hold on to the handlebars?

Maybe there was still time to get out of it.

I waited until Jack had gone upstairs, and then called Grandma.

"Hello?" She sounded groggy.

"Did I wake you?"

"Of course you woke me. Don't you know it's Sunday?"

"Sorry."

"This had better be a matter of life or death."

"My hands are sore."

"And you rang to tell me that?"

"I took part in a tug-of-war yesterday, and my hands haven't recovered."

"I should care about that because—?"

"I'm not sure I'll be able to do the bike ride. I won't be able to grip the handlebars."

"Typical! The youth of today has no backbone. It's a tandem. I can't take part in the bike ride without you, so you'd better be there."

"What about my hands?"

"Wear gloves."

With that, the line went dead. I knew I could rely on Grandma to be sympathetic.

***

When we arrived at Wash Point where the competition was being held, I was pleased to see that the fence, which had once made a stretch of the river inaccessible, had now been removed. The council had taken it down after I'd helped to shut down the factory responsible for the dangerous trade in pixie-to-human transformations.

"Jill! Jack! Over here!" Kathy called from the other riverbank. Lizzie was at her side.

I led the way over the footbridge, to join them.

"Where are Peter and Mikey?" I said.

"They've been allocated pegs downstream."

"What do they need pegs for?"

"That's what they call the spot on the river that each competitor is allocated. I thought Lizzie and I had better wait here until you arrived."

"Is Mikey nervous?"

"He wasn't until he got here. We had no idea that there would only be two entrants in the under-ten class: Mikey and a boy called Simon. The other boy has been fishing for three years, so he's much more experienced than Mikey. As soon as we got here, the little monster started taunting Mikey. Finishing halfway down a field of ten wouldn't be so bad, but with only two of them in it, Mikey is either going to end up the winner or the loser. And, I fear the latter is more likely."

"He'll be okay. Kids are pretty resilient."

"I hope you're right. Shall we go and see them?"

"Sure. Lead the way."

As the four of us began to walk along the riverbank, Lizzie grabbed my hand.

"Caroline still hasn't come back, Auntie Jill. I'm worried that something bad has happened to her."

"I'm sure it hasn't. I still think she's on holiday. A lot of people go away for two weeks. I'm sure she'll be back in a few more days."

"Promise?"

What was I meant to say to that? "Err—yeah. I promise."

I had better be right, otherwise Lizzie would be devastated, and I'd be to blame.

"How's it going, you two?" Jack said when we reached the stretch of riverbank where both Peter and Mikey were seated. "Caught much yet?"

"Give us a chance." Peter grinned. "We've only just started."

"What about you, Mikey? Any bites yet?"

"No. I'm going to lose."

Kathy gave me a look, and then turned to Mikey. "I've already told you, Mikey. It doesn't matter who wins, as long as you have fun."

"It won't be fun if Simon beats me." He glared at the opposite riverbank. Only then did I realise there was another young boy seated almost directly across from us. I was no judge of such things, but his fishing tackle looked much more elaborate than Mikey's, and certainly much more expensive.

"Caught anything yet, loser?" Simon shouted at Mikey.

"Ignore him." Kathy put her hand on Mikey's shoulder.

"Where are his parents?" I said.

"That's his dad, just up there." Kathy gestured to a man seated a few yards downstream from Simon. The man looked like he'd bought all of his clothes from Fishermen Chic.

"Why doesn't he tell his kid not to be so horrible?"

"That's Sandy," Peter chipped in. "He's as bad as his son. A prize prat if ever there was one."

As promised, Kathy had brought along a picnic basket. Halfway through the morning, Peter and Mikey left their pegs, and joined us for drinks and snacks.

"How's it going, Mikey?" I asked.

"Rubbish. I've only caught three tiddlers."

"Three isn't bad."

"I've seen Simon land at least six, and two of them were big ones."

"I'm sure things will pick up later. How do they decide who the winner is? Is it whoever catches the most fish?"

"No," Peter said. "It's the overall weight that matters."

"When does the competition finish?"

"There's another two hours to go."

"What about you, Peter?" Jack asked. "How are you doing?

"Terrible. I've only caught one so far."

"See, Mikey," Kathy said. "You're doing better than your dad."

"I'm still going to lose."

As it grew closer to the midday finish time, Simon became more and more cocky and obnoxious.

"Hey, loser. How many fish have you caught now?"

"Call that little thing a fish? Ha, ha, ha."

"I'm going to keep the trophy in my bedroom."

Mikey was close to tears, but he didn't rise to the bait; he just kept on fishing.

With about ten minutes to go before the end of the competition, Mikey's float bobbed down in the water; he had a bite. It was time to show Simon that being obnoxious doesn't pay, so I cast a spell to make the fish on Mikey's line bigger.

Much bigger.

For a moment, I thought I'd overdone it because he struggled to land the monster fish, but eventually he managed to get it into his keepnet. On the other riverbank, Simon had caught a small fish of his own, so he hadn't seen Mikey's catch.

Once the competition had ended, all of the competitors gathered by the footbridge. The judges weighed everyone's catch, and then returned the fish to the river. It then took almost thirty minutes for the judges to announce the winners in the various classes. Needless to say, Peter came nowhere, but he seemed to take it in good part.

"And now we come to the under-ten class. In first place, with a total catch of nine pounds, is Mikey Brooks."

Simon's face fell. "That's not fair, Dad." He buried his head in his father's chest. "I should have won," he blubbered.

"Go on, Mikey." Kathy gave him a little nudge. "Go and get your cup."

"That last fish that Mikey landed was unbelievable," Jack said, as we drove home. "He was miles behind until he caught that."

"I know. Did you see his little face when he got the cup?"

"He was chuffed to bits, and so he should have been."

"I just hope he doesn't expect to catch whoppers like that every time."

***

We'd no sooner got back home than I had to leave again.

"Where are you off to?" Jack said.

"I thought I mentioned it this morning. I have to meet a client at the office."

"I'm pretty sure you didn't mention it. On a Sunday afternoon?"

"It was the only time he could make it. I shouldn't be long." I shot out of the door before he could ask any more awkward questions.

There was no need to drive all the way into Washbridge, so I pulled into the first layby I came to, and from there, magicked myself over to Candlefield.

"Why are you wearing gloves?" Grandma was standing next to our tandem.

"I told you when I called earlier that my hands are sore from yesterday's tug-of-war."

"Just wait until you have old wizened hands like mine." She waved her bony fingers in my face. "Then you'll have something to complain about."

"Where exactly does the bike ride take place?"

"They've closed off the market place and surrounding roads. The route is clearly sign-posted."

"How long is the course?"

"Twenty-five circuits."

"That sounds a long way."

"Stop complaining and get on the bike."

I climbed onto the front seat.

"What do you think you're doing?" She glared at me.

"You told me to get on."

"You should be on the rear."

"Are you sure? Is your eyesight up to this?"

"There's nothing wrong with my eyesight. I'll have you

know that I have twenty-twenty vision. Now get on the back, will you?"

"We don't have to rush around the course, do we? I'm still tired from the charity sports competition."

"You poor little petal. Don't worry. It isn't a race, so even you should be able to cope."

Thank goodness. At least I'd be able to sit back, relax and let Grandma do all the hard work.

"Hello, Mirabel."

The familiar but unwelcome voice took us both by surprise. Ma Chivers had just pulled her tandem level with ours. Seated on the back was Cyril.

"What do you think you're doing, Chivers?" Grandma said. "This ride will kill you."

"I wouldn't be so sure. Care for a wager on who finishes first?"

"Easy money. How about ten pieces of silver?"

"Make it twenty."

"Done."

Oh bum!

"Grandma." I leaned forward to whisper in her ear. "I'm not sure this is a good idea."

Just then, a klaxon sounded, and we were off.

Where Grandma got her energy from, I'll never know. We sped around the course at breakneck speed; it took me all my time just to stay on the bike.

"Pedal faster!" she yelled, as we fell behind Ma Chivers and Cyril.

With only one lap to go, I was totally spent, and we were still trailing behind Ma Chivers. I didn't care; I just wanted it to be over. As we approached the final bend,

Grandma threw the bike so low onto its side that I scraped my knee on the floor. The risky manoeuvre had the desired effect because we slipped past Ma Chivers and Cyril on the inside.

Moments later we crossed the finish line in first place.

I climbed off the bike and slumped in a heap on the floor; my legs had turned to jelly. Not so for Grandma. She rushed over to Ma Chivers, and held out her hand. I couldn't hear what was said between them, but if Ma Chivers' expression was anything to go by, she was not a good loser.

"Easy money." Grandma rattled the coins in her cupped hands.

Grandma had gone home, skipping as she went, but I was still trying to find enough energy to magic myself back to Washbridge. I was sitting with my back against a tree when I heard Ma Chivers' voice.

"That was your fault, Cyril. You should never have let her slip past us like that."

"Sorry, Ma. I was peddling as fast as I could."

"Not fast enough. I'll never hear the end of this from Mirabel."

"You'll get your own back soon enough when your shop opens."

"You're right. Let's see how she likes it when all of her customers desert her for YarnStormers." She cackled.

I waited until they'd left, and then magicked myself back to the car in Washbridge. I had to warn Kathy.

She picked up on the first ring.

"Jill? We've only just got back in. We stopped off for a

celebratory dinner on the way home. Mikey is so excited. Did you see the size of that fish he caught?"

"Yeah, it was fantastic. Look, the reason I've called is to tell you that you can't take that job with YarnStormers."

"Why not? Did you let it slip to your grandmother? Has she told you to call me?"

"No. I haven't said anything to her."

"So what's this all about?"

"I've found out who owns YarnStormers, and she is seriously bad news."

"Who is it?"

"Her name is Chivers. If you think Grandma is bad, you haven't seen anything yet. Chivers is pure evil."

"How do you know her?"

"I — err — I've had business dealings with her."

"What kind of business dealings?"

"She — err — almost made a client of mine bankrupt. She's a real piece of work, Kathy. You have to turn down the job."

"Are you absolutely sure about this?"

"One hundred percent."

"Okay. I guess there's no point in jumping out of the frying pan into the fire. It's disappointing because the extra money would have been nice."

"It's the right decision, Kathy. You have to trust me on this one."

"Okay. Thanks for warning me."

I'd no sooner finished on that call than my phone rang.

"Is that Ms Gooder?"

"Speaking."

"It's Kitty Landers. I've had a long chat with Conrad, and he's agreed to speak to you on the phone."

"That's great. Thank you."

"Don't thank me. Just prove my son is innocent. Help me to get him out of prison."

"When will he call me?"

"It should be sometime tomorrow."

"Okay. Thanks again."

"You were quick." Jack was lying on the sofa; he had a glass of beer on the coffee table beside him.

"I told you it wouldn't take me long."

"What on earth did you do to your knee?"

"Oh? I—err—tripped on my way back to the car."

"You're so clumsy. Shall I get you something to put on it?"

"No. Just give me a kiss. That will make it better."

"I can do much better than that."

Chapter 18

"The new ballroom opens tonight," Jack said, in between spoonfuls of muesli.

"So it does."

"Exciting, isn't it?"

Yawn. "Very."

"We really ought to drop in. Then we can say we were there on day one."

"I thought we'd agreed that it would be much too busy on opening day?"

"If you called your grandmother, I'd bet she'd sort something out for us."

"You really don't know Grandma, do you?"

"Couldn't she sneak us in the back way or something?"

"I'm not going to ask her. It isn't the 'getting in' that's the problem. The place will be wall-to-wall with woolly waltzers. You won't be able to move in there. And besides, I'm up to my neck in work at the moment. I can't spare the time to go dancing."

"Okay, but we'll go as soon as things have died down. Agreed?"

"Absolutely. Just as soon as the novelty has worn off, we'll be there." Ten years should just about do it.

My phone rang; Caller ID showed that it was Constance Bowler.

"Hi." I made my way upstairs because I didn't want to have to explain to Jack why I was talking to a ghost police chief.

"I'm sorry to call so early, Jill, but I have meetings all day, and I wanted to catch you first."

"No problem. Have you located Caroline?"

"Yes. I have her address. Do you have a pen handy?"

I scribbled the address down, thanked Constance, and made my way back downstairs.

"Who was that?" Jack was rinsing his bowl.

"Just a client."

"They're keen, aren't they?"

"I told you I was busy."

***

Even after all this time, Candlefield still had a 'magical' feel about it. I couldn't exactly put into words what I meant by 'magical', but essentially it always felt 'other worldly'.

The streets and houses were quite different to anything in the human world. In the early days, I'd found it very confusing when travelling around the sup world because the distance between two locations seemed to count for nothing. It might take me ten minutes to walk a particular route one day, but then take twice as long the next time. Distances in Candlefield seemed somehow to be 'elastic'. Another thing that had blown my mind at first, but which I'd grown accustomed to, was the fact that I never needed a map or street signs to find my way around. In Candlefield, I simply had to think of the location I wanted to visit, and then start walking. Magic did the rest.

GT was different in almost every respect. The houses and streets resembled much more closely those in the human world. The distance between two locations did not vary from day to day; it was fixed. And relying on magic to find your way around was going to get you only one place: Lostville.

"Morning," I said to the slim, tall man behind the counter of the Ghost Town News and Convenience Store.

He did the usual double take. "You're that witch. I've heard rumours about you, but I didn't believe them."

"They're true."

"So I see. I'm Bob Kitecatcher." He offered his hand. "I'm very pleased to make your acquaintance."

"Jill Gooder."

"I thought your hand would feel different," he said.

"Different how?"

"I don't know. Silly, really. Anyhow, what can I get for you?"

"I'm new here, as you know. To be honest, I'm having difficulty finding my way around. Do you by any chance have a map of Ghost Town?"

"GT is a big place. There are numerous maps."

"Of course. I should have realised."

"What you need is the GT map app."

"There's an app?"

"Of course. Why wouldn't there be?" He took out his phone, and showed me the screen which was full of apps.

"I suppose I expected this place to be the same as Candlefield. There's no internet there."

"Where's Candlefield?"

"In the sup world."

"Oh, right. I've never heard it called by name before. I didn't even realise there were such things as sups until I arrived here. It's surprising what you learn when you're dead."

"I guess so."

"We have internet and smart phones here."

"Thank goodness. That's the one thing about Candlefield that drives me crazy. Do you think I'd be able to run the map app on my phone?"

"I don't see why not. Pass me your phone, and I'll install it for you."

I did as he asked.

"Hmm? I'll need to install GT Play first." He fiddled around for a couple of minutes. "That seems to have worked okay. Now, let me try and install the map app." Another couple of minutes of fiddling. "That's it. Take a look."

He demonstrated the app, which worked pretty much the same as map apps I had used in the human world.

"Thank you so much, Bob."

"It was my pleasure. Is there anything else I can get for you?"

"No, thanks. I should be okay now."

"Do call in again. I'd love to catch up with what's happening in the human world."

"Okay, bye, and thanks again."

The app was great. After I'd typed in the address that Constance had given to me, a map and directions appeared. According to the on-screen info, it would take me fifteen minutes on foot. Apparently, it was only five minutes by bus, but I had no idea where to catch one, or how often they ran. On a whim, I tried to magic myself there, but nothing happened. Did that mean my magic wouldn't work in GT? To find out, I tried the 'invisible' spell, and that seemed to work just fine. Weird! Maybe some spells worked in GT, and others didn't. This was going to be a learning process.

Either I was a very slow walker, or the app wasn't particularly accurate because it took me almost twenty-five minutes to reach Caroline's house; an end terraced with a small, but beautifully maintained front garden.

I knocked on the door; it opened so quickly it made me jump.

"Sorry if I scared you." The woman who answered the door had curlers in her hair. "I was just coming out to look for the cat. You haven't seen her, have you?"

"No, sorry."

"Can I help you?"

I found it curious how different people reacted to seeing a sup. Some were visibly shocked while others, such as this woman, seemed barely to notice.

"Does Caroline live here?"

"Caroline is my daughter. Who are you?"

"My name is Jill Gooder. I live in the human world."

"You're not dead, then?"

"Dead? Err—no."

"I didn't realise that the non-dead were able to visit us now, but then I don't keep up with the news. What do you want with Caroline?"

"My niece goes to school in Washbridge. That's in the human world."

"I know where Washbridge is. I used to live there before I came here."

"Sorry. Anyway, my niece and Caroline are—err—friends, I suppose."

"What's your niece's name?"

"Lizzie."

"Why didn't you say so before? Caroline is always talking about Lizzie. She says they are BFFs—whatever that means."

"Best friends forever."

"Right. Of course."

"Is Caroline okay?"

"She's been laid up in bed with the flu, but she's a lot better now. She's been worried that Lizzie might think she'd abandoned her."

"I told Lizzie that Caroline was probably on holiday, but I wanted to check for myself."

"Why don't you come in, and see her?"

"Is that okay?"

"Of course. She's over the worst now. Come in."

I followed her into the lounge where a little girl was lying on the sofa, watching TV.

"Turn that down, Caroline. You have a visitor."

Caroline muted the TV.

"I'm Jill. Lizzie is my niece."

"Lizzie?" Her face lit up. "Is she okay?"

"She's fine, but she's been a little worried about you."

"I've had the flu, but I'm better now. I can go out again tomorrow, can't I, Mum?"

"Yes, you should be able to."

"That's great." I smiled. "I'll let Lizzie know."

"Would you give her something from me?" Caroline held up a small beanie ghost.

"Are you sure?"

"Yes. I bought it especially for her."

"That's very kind, thank you. It was nice to meet you, Caroline, I'm glad you're feeling better."

Her mother showed me back to the door. "Thank you for calling around."

"No problem. Do you mind if I ask you something?"

"What's that?"

"What connection does Caroline have to Lizzie's school?"

"It's the school she used to attend before the accident. She and I were in a car crash, and—err—well—we didn't make it."

"I'm so sorry."

"Don't be. We're really happy here, and Caroline still gets to visit her old school."

"Tell Caroline thanks again for the beanie."

***

I was starving, and would have killed for a muffin, but I wasn't sure what kind of reception I would get at Spooky Wooky. The last time I'd seen Harry and Larry, I'd told them that their suspicions regarding Stewey Dewey were completely wrong. Would they still be upset with me? My muffin cravings were too strong to ignore, so I decided to take my chances, and hope that the two guys wouldn't refuse to serve me.

"Jill! I'm so glad you've called in." Harry greeted me with a huge smile.

That was promising.

"We were going to call you later." Larry joined him behind the counter.

"I wasn't sure if the two of you would be speaking to me or not."

"We owe you an apology," Harry said.

Larry nodded. "We were so angry about what happened that we jumped to conclusions. We'd heard that Stewey was at the scene of the fire, and had been questioned by the police, so we just assumed he was behind it."

"That's right," Harry said. "But since you put us right, we've done a lot of research, and we clearly misjudged the poor man. He tried to save us, and has lost everything since then."

"He is in a bad way."

"We want to put this right," Harry said. "We've discussed it, and we've agreed that we owe Stewey that much."

"How do you mean: *put it right*?"

"We need to let him see that we're doing okay, so he doesn't continue to live his life blaming himself for our deaths."

"Hold on. Are you saying what I think you're saying?"

"We want to speak to Stewey."

"But to do that, he'd have to let you attach yourselves to him. I can't see him doing that."

"He might if you speak to him."

"I suppose I could try, but to be honest, he's not in a very good place at the moment. If I start talking about ghosts, that might just push him over the edge."

"Please, Jill. Will you at least try? We've messed this up badly, and we want to put things right."

"Okay, I'll give it a go, but I'm making no promises. I'll need something from you first, though."

"What's that?"

"A blueberry muffin and a caramel latte."

"Coming up. And they're on the house."

Music to my ears.

***

After I'd finished my freebie muffin and coffee, I magicked myself back to the high street in Washbridge because I wanted to pick up a sandwich.

What? It was for my lunch, later. Sheesh.

As I was walking towards my office, I happened across Norman, who was standing outside his shop.

"Morning, Norman."

Wait for it. Any moment now.

"Oh? Yeah. Morning."

There you go.

"I'm glad I've seen you, Jill."

"You are?" I was just amazed that he'd remembered my name.

"I wanted to thank you for telling me about WashBets and Tonya. We went out the other night, and we really hit it off."

"That's great. Does she share your interest in bottle tops?"

"No. She thinks they're silly, but she loves maths—just like me."

"You like maths?"

"Yeah. After bottle tops, it's my biggest interest."

Who da thought it? "That's good to hear, Norman."

"I feel like I owe you one, Jill. If there's anything I can do in return, please let me know."

"Now you come to mention it, there is one thing."

***

Jules and Gilbert were in the office.

"Hello, you two."

"Gilbert has only popped in to bring me a sandwich for lunch."

"That's okay. I'm glad I caught you together. I have something for you." I took the tickets from my bag and handed them to Gilbert.

"ToppersCon tickets?" He was beside himself with excitement. "Look, Jules!"

"Great." She seemed rather less enthusiastic.

"Where did you get these?" Gilbert asked. "They're like gold dust."

"From Norman who owns Top Of The World. He and I are old friends."

"Thank you so much." Gilbert gave me a hug. "I suppose I'd better get going. See you later, Jules."

"Bye."

As soon as he was out of the door, Jules glared at me.

"What?"

"Thanks very much, Jill. Now I have to go to that stupid convention."

Whoops. Snigger.

Chapter 19

Winky was dressed as a cowboy.

The most worrying aspect of that was the fact that I wasn't even slightly surprised. I'd now got to a point where finding my cat dressed as a cowboy no longer affected me. What did that say about my life?

In the centre of the office, was a camera mounted on a tripod. I watched, mesmerised, as Winky stood in front of the sofa, and then pressed a button on his little gizmo, to take a photo of himself.

"Go on then. I'll bite. What's with the cowboy outfit?"

"This? Nothing. I just fancied a change. How do I look?"

"Pretty good, actually." Credit where it was due. The cowboy-look definitely suited him.

My phone rang. When I answered, I was met with an automated, robotic voice.

"This is a call from HMP Westerton. Are you prepared to accept this call from inmate Conrad Landers? Press '1' for yes or '2' for no."

I pressed '1'.

"Hello? Is that Jill Gooder?"

"Speaking."

"It's Conrad Landers. My mother said you wanted to speak to me."

"That's right. Thanks for calling. I'm working on a missing person case—Angie Potts."

"I remember the case. I was questioned about it. Why are you working on that twenty years on?"

"Her mother is still desperate to know what happened to her."

"I don't see how I can help. I didn't have anything to do with it; just like I didn't have anything to do with Patty Lake's murder."

"I understand you were offered some kind of plea bargain?"

"I turned it down. They wanted me to plead guilty to something I hadn't done. I never laid a hand on Patty."

"You did date her, though?"

"Not for long, and it was months before she was killed. She dumped me."

"Why?"

"For someone else, but I don't know who. Look, the only reason I was convicted was because her blood-stained top was found in my locker at the garage where I worked. I'm not a violent man. I would never hurt anyone."

"You must see why the discovery of the blood-stained top would make you a prime suspect?"

"Of course I can, but I didn't put it in there."

"Who do you think did?"

"I've no idea. I've had twenty years to think about it, but I still don't have a clue."

"How did you meet Patty?"

"She was a receptionist at the garage for a while."

"What exactly did the police ask you about Angie Potts?"

"They didn't ask many questions. They more or less insinuated that I must have killed her, and said because I was going to prison for the rest of my life anyway, that I might as well confess."

"What did you say?"

"What do you think I said? I told them to do one. That's

the problem with the police. They're more interested in locking someone up—anyone—than they are in finding the person who actually committed the crime. Patty Lake's murderer is still out there, and who knows, he could have killed again. Maybe he killed Angie Potts too."

"Did you know Angie?"

"No. I'd never heard of her until the police questioned me about her."

Just then, the automated voice came on the line to warn us we had only thirty seconds left.

"Thanks for talking to me, Conrad."

"No problem. I hope you turn up something that will help me."

I had no idea what to make of any of that. He didn't sound like a guilty man, and there can't be many murderers who wouldn't have jumped at the chance of a plea bargain in his position. Unfortunately, nothing he had told me had got me any closer to finding Angie Potts.

"Jill." Jules appeared in the doorway. "I have someone out there who wants to see you. She says her name is Lolly."

Great! That was all I needed. "Give me a minute, and then bring her through, would you?"

"Hey, Cowboy Joe," I called to Winky.

"You called, ma'am?" He tipped his Stetson.

"Have you had any more feedback from your guys?"

"You mean my posse?"

"Yeah. Any more info on the Lolly Jolly situation?"

"Her boyfriend hasn't been anywhere near her over the weekend."

"Right. It looks like the problem has resolved itself. Lolly will be pleased."

"Jill!" Lolly was wearing her usual lollipop-themed attire. "Thanks for seeing me."

"No problem."

She did a double take at Winky. "Why is your cat dressed like a cowboy?"

"They were all out of pirate costumes."

"Huh?"

"It's just a thing I like doing. Dressing up the cat."

"Right?" Lolly took a seat. "I'm back because my ex has been at it again. Every time I look around, there he is."

"Are you saying that your boyfriend has been stalking you again?"

"Yes. It's getting worse and worse. Did you follow him like you said you would? Where else has he been? What's he been doing? Has he been seen with anyone else?"

"I'm really sorry, Lolly, but I've been run off my feet. I didn't get a chance to follow him."

"You promised you would, Jill."

"I know, and I'm sorry."

"Can you do it now?"

"I'm still very busy."

"Please, Jill. For the sake of our friendship."

"Okay. I'll try to get onto it this week."

"Thanks, Jill." She stood up. "I want to know everything he's up to."

"Okay."

"Bye, cowboy," she called to Winky, as she made for the door.

"Lolly, you haven't forgotten about my retainer, have

you? It's three hundred pounds."

"Of course not, but I don't have my purse with me just now. I'll sort you out next time."

As soon as she'd gone, I turned to Winky. "I thought your posse said her boyfriend had been nowhere near her?"

"He hasn't. She's lying. Even I can see that, and I'm just a cat. A cool, cowboy cat it's true, but still a cat."

My phone rang; it was Ella Brand.

"Jill, I have fantastic news."

"Alfie?"

"Yes. He's back. When I went into the shed this morning, he was in his cage."

"How is he?"

"He seems okay. His feathers looked a shade lighter, but that was probably just my imagination. It's so wonderful to have him back."

"I'm really thrilled for you."

"Thanks for your help, Jill."

"I didn't really do anything."

"Still, you must send me a bill for the time you spent on this."

"Okay."

I had no intention of doing that. The charity had hardly any money as it was, and I didn't want Ella to pay me out of her own pocket when she'd already poured so much money into the bird sanctuary. Graham Clawson and the OSA had come through for Alfie. Hopefully, they would be able to cover for him until such time as he was up and about again.

***

I'd promised to help the twins to choose a fish tank for Cuppy C. I hadn't seen them since the Timmy/Tammy fiasco, and I fully expected them to be in a deep, dark depression.

I couldn't have been any more wrong.

"Hi, Jill!" Amber beamed.

"Muffin, Jill?" Pearl was just as upbeat.

Colour me confused.

"You two are very chipper."

"Why wouldn't we be? We're excited about picking our fish tank."

"I thought that maybe last Friday would still be playing on your minds?"

"Friday? Oh, you mean the book signing?"

"Yeah. The shop was so full that I couldn't get inside, but I did bump into Timmy."

"What a mix up." Amber laughed.

"I'm very impressed by how well you're both taking this. It can't have been easy when you discovered it wasn't Tammy?"

"We thought we were in trouble at first, but that was until the audience saw Timmy's book."

"A Hundred Things to do with Asparagus?"

"Yeah. It turns out that the culinary contingent of Candlefield have been starved of good asparagus-related books. Timmy had sold out within an hour. He had to take the names and addresses of those who missed out."

"Wasn't anyone peeved because it wasn't Tammy Winestock?"

"If they were, they didn't say anything to us. They were

more interested in who we'd be booking next."

"That's fantastic."

"Would you like a muffin?"

"Does a cat like to dress up as a cowboy?"

"Sorry?"

"Never mind. Yes. I'll take the usual blueberry and a cup of tea, please."

While Amber was getting my order, I spotted Mindy, sitting by the window.

"There you go." Amber passed me the muffin.

"I see Mindy's here?" I said in a hushed voice.

"She came in the other day, to apologise for all the stuff that has gone on between us. She asked if we'd mind if she came in from time to time. We could hardly say no, could we? She seems so down in the dumps."

Amber was right. Mindy looked as though she'd just lost the winning lottery ticket.

"Do you mind if I join you, Mindy?"

She looked up, and forced a smile. "Sure."

"How are things?"

"Okay, I guess."

"You've finished with Miles?"

"Yes, but he doesn't want to accept it. He keeps pestering me to get back with him."

"Will you?"

"Never. I'm done with that man."

"Where are you living?"

"With my sister, but don't tell Miles. I don't want him to come around there."

"I won't say a thing. And look, if he keeps bothering you, let me know, and I'll put him straight."

"Thanks, Jill. Anyway, I suppose I'd better get going."

As soon as I'd finished my tea and muffin, the twins were standing by my table.

"Are you ready, Jill?"

"It looks like you two are."

"We're really excited about choosing the fish tank."

"Have you taken measurements?"

"Yeah. We've got all the info we need. Come on, let's get going."

"Where are we going, anyway?"

"Everything Aquatic."

***

"Good afternoon, ladies." The man behind the counter greeted us with a smile, and a flourish of the hand. "I'm Bill Fishman, the owner. What can I do for you today?"

"Fishman? You don't by any chance know the owner of Everything Rodent, do you?"

"I don't think so."

"You'll never believe this. He owns Everything Rodent, and his name is Bill Ratman. And you own Everything Aquatic, and your name is Bill Fishman."

"So?" He shrugged.

"Surely, you see the coincidence?"

"You mean because we're both called Bill? It's a pretty common name."

"No, not that. I mean—"

"Jill! You're embarrassing us." Amber glared at me. "Stop harassing the man."

"We need a large tank to put in our tea room," Amber said. "My sister and I own Cuppy C."

"I know it well. Your cupcakes are to die for."

That brought a smile to the twins' faces.

He continued, "The large tanks are down at the far end of the shop. Feel free to browse, and give me a shout if you have any questions."

"Look at these!" Amber's face lit up when she spotted the giant tanks.

"I think you want the ones over there." I pointed to some slightly smaller ones to our right.

"No, these look perfect." Pearl joined her sister.

"Are you sure? They're huge. You'd better check the dimensions."

Amber had at least had the foresight to bring a tape measure with her. She held one end while Pearl walked to the far side of the tank. "Ninety."

"That should be okay."

"Are you sure?" I said. "It looks awfully big."

"Positive. Let's just check the width." Pearl took the other end of the tape again. "Fifty-five."

"Perfect." Amber gave the thumbs up.

I stood back and took a long look at the tank. I just couldn't see how it would possibly fit inside the shop. "Are you sure those dimensions are correct?"

"Absolutely. They've been checked and double-checked."

Just then, Bill Fishman came over to join us. "Seen anything you like?"

"We'll take this one." Pearl tapped the glass.

"The Supreme? An excellent choice if I might say so. That will give your customers something to talk about."

"It's very big," I said, but by now, no one was listening.

Chapter 20

Something about the Lolly Jolly situation didn't ring true. On the one hand, Lolly insisted that her boyfriend had continued to stalk her, but on the other, Winky's posse said he'd been nowhere near her. They couldn't both be right. If it had been just Winky following the boyfriend, I might have had my doubts. That cat was easily distracted. But it had been his whole gang; they surely couldn't all have got it wrong, could they?

Although I hadn't told Lolly of my intentions, it seemed pointless to waste time following the boyfriend any longer. If he really was stalking her, then I needed to put a stop to it. A quick word in his shell-like ought to do the trick.

He was living in a bedsit in Westcliff House. From the outside, the place looked run-down; inside it was ten times worse. The lift was out of commission, and if the dog-eared notice taped to the door was anything to go by, it had been for a long time. Several of the lights on the stairs were out, and many of the windows were boarded up. Inevitably, he lived on the ninth floor, so by the time I reached his door, I was pretty much gasping for air.

I pressed the doorbell, and to my surprise, it actually worked.

"Yes?" The young man who answered the door was wearing jeans, and a string vest.

"Nick Long?" I managed to say, in between wheezes.

"Yes?"

"I'd like to ask you a few questions."

"Who are you? What's this all about? If it's to do with

the rent, I'll have it next Friday."

"I'm not here about the rent. I wanted to talk to you about Lolly Jolly."

"That psycho? Are you a friend of hers?"

"Yes — err — no — I'm a private investigator."

"I don't want anything to do with her. Does she know where I live?"

This was not the response I'd been expecting.

"Do you think I could get a drink of water?" My throat felt like it was on fire.

"Sure. You'd better come inside."

To my surprise, the rooms were tidy. Dirty and grubby, but very tidy.

"Thanks." I took a drink. "How long has the lift been out?"

"Ever since I've been here. You said you wanted to talk about Lolly?"

"I believe you are — err — were her boyfriend?"

"We went out for a short time. No more than a month. That's all."

"How did you meet?"

"It was one of those dating apps. I noticed her home town was Washbridge. I was born here too, so I thought we'd at least have something in common to talk about. Biggest mistake of my life."

"It didn't work out, then?"

"I knew after the first date that I'd made a mistake, but I couldn't shake her. She drove me crazy with her antics, and she was always singing stupid songs. And of course, she never had any money. Every time we went out, she'd either forgotten or lost her purse. In the end, I couldn't stand it any longer, so I told her it was over."

"And that was it?"

"I wish. She wouldn't take no for an answer. She phoned and texted me non-stop. She'd turn up at my place of work, and at my flat at all hours of the day. She used to follow me everywhere. In the end, I couldn't take any more, so I moved back here. But then, the other day I saw her in Washbridge. She must have followed me. Look, if you're her friend, won't you please tell her to leave me alone."

Instinctively, I knew he wasn't lying. Lolly had wanted me to follow him not to check if he was stalking her, but to gather as much information about his movements as possible. She'd used me.

"Thanks for the drink. I'm sorry to have bothered you."

"What are you going to tell Lolly?"

"Do you still have friends in London? Is there anywhere you could stay down there?"

"Yeah, a few. I never really wanted to leave."

"Good. Pack a bag, and get the next train down there."

"But she'll just follow me again."

"No, she won't. I'll see to that."

***

As I walked back along the high street, I was still trying to get my head around what Lolly had done. She'd lied in order to get me to follow her poor ex, who was desperate to escape her clutches. That young lady deserved everything that was coming to her.

Suddenly, my attention was caught by some kind of altercation outside Betty's shop, She Sells. Being the civic-minded individual that I was, and definitely not because I was just nosey, I decided to find out what was going on.

Rolling around on the ground, fighting, were two young men. I recognised the one in the scruffy leather jacket; it was Betty's new boyfriend, Sid. I didn't recognise the smartly dressed young man who seemed to be getting the worst of the encounter. Looking on, was a photographer, and a woman holding a notepad and pen.

"Jill! You have to stop them." Betty appeared at my side.

"What's going on?"

"Do you remember I told you that I was going to hire a male escort to do the profile for Crustacean Monthly?"

"Is that him?" I pointed to the guy on the ground with Sid.

"Yes, that's Tarquin. We were just about to get our photo taken when Sid turned up. Can't you do something?"

It was obvious that no one else was going to step in, so if I didn't intervene, Tarquin would probably need a trip to A&E. I cast the 'power' spell, grabbed hold of Sid's leather jacket, and pulled him off Tarquin.

"Let me go!" Sid flailed around, but he was never going to escape my grip.

"Tarquin! Get out of here!"

Tarquin didn't need telling twice. He was on his feet, and legging it down the street within seconds. Only when he was out of sight, did I release Sid.

"What's going on?" The reporter looked more than a little puzzled.

"Just a mix-up," I said. "This is Betty's boyfriend. Why don't you go ahead and take your photos?" I pushed Sid towards Betty who scowled at me.

"Smile for the camera, Betty," I said, and then went on my way. But not before making a mental note to look out for the next edition of Crustacean Monthly. That was one profile I couldn't wait to see.

I'd been so distracted by the goings on outside She Sells that I hadn't noticed the long queue on the opposite side of the street. It was only when I spotted Mrs V and Armi that I realised they must be queuing for the Ever ballroom, which was due to open at five pm. I walked over to have a word with them.

"You two are going to have a long wait."

"It will be worth it, won't it Armi?" she said.

"Most certainly."

"Aren't you and Jack coming?"

"I wanted to, but Jack had to work. Maybe another night. Have fun you two."

***

I didn't want to get home too early because I was worried Jack might decide we should go to the ballroom.

"Jill?" Kathy had a potato peeler in her hand when she came to the door. "Was I expecting you?"

"No, but I didn't think I needed an appointment."

"Come in. I'm just in the middle of peeling the spuds. You can help, if you like?"

"That would be fun, but I was hoping to have a word with Lizzie."

"She's upstairs."

"How's she doing?"

"She's still rather quiet. I've asked her several times what the problem is, but she says there's nothing wrong."

"This might cheer her up." I took the beanie ghost out of my bag.

"You bought that for her?"

"Don't sound so shocked. I am her auntie."

"Why don't you take it up to her? Hopefully that will do the trick."

I knocked on Lizzie's bedroom door, and popped my head inside. "Can I come in?"

Lizzie was sitting on the bed, reading a book. "Yeah."

"Are you still feeling glum?"

"Caroline still hasn't come back."

"I have good news about that."

"You do?" Her face lit up. "What?"

"I've spoken to Caroline. She's had the flu, but she's feeling much better now. She should be back within a few days."

"Are you sure about that, or are you just saying that to make me feel better?"

"No, I promise." I brought the beanie from behind my back. "She asked me to give you this."

"Caroline sent it for me?" Lizzie grabbed the beanie, and then jumped down from the bed, and ran out of the room. When I caught up with her, she was showing her new toy to her mum.

"Lizzie tells me Caroline sent it for her?"

"That's right." I winked at Kathy who had just finished peeling the spuds. Shame. I was just about to offer to help.

"What's all the noise?" I looked out the kitchen window. Normally this neighbourhood was very quiet, but I could hear loud music coming from somewhere close by.

"It's next door but one."

"Isn't that the elderly couple?"

"Yes. The Connellys are as good as gold usually; we never hear a peep from them. They've gone away on holiday, and it looks as though they've let their house while they're away. Two young couples moved in yesterday, and it's been non-stop music ever since then."

"I'm surprised they would trust their house to strangers?"

"Me too. They're both very house-proud. I reckon the place will be wrecked by the time they come back. Still, they've only themselves to blame. They must have figured they could make a little extra cash."

"Do they have a cat, by any chance?"

"Yeah. A big black thing. I think its name is Oscar or something like that. Why?"

"No reason."

Hmm? I was beginning to smell a cat.

***

Stewey Dewey looked just as bad as the last time I'd seen him.

"You again?" He tried to close the door, but I wedged my foot in the gap.

"I just need a few minutes of your time."

"I don't want to talk about the fire again. I've said all I have to say."

"Please. This won't take long, and then I promise you'll never see me again."

He hesitated, but then stepped aside to let me in. The exterior of the house was bad enough, but it was nothing compared to the interior. He led the way through to what had probably once been the lounge, but which now resembled a tip. If there was any furniture in the room, it had long since been buried under rubbish. The smell made me want to retch.

"What do you want?"

"When I was here before, I got the impression that you've never really got over the fire?"

"You think?"

"You seem to blame yourself for Harry and Larry's deaths."

"I should have got them out. I could hear them shouting for help." He hesitated. "I still can."

"Would it help you to know that they don't blame you?"

"Is that what you came here for?" He scoffed. "To tell me it wasn't my fault? Don't you think I've tried to tell myself that a million times? It doesn't help."

"What if *they* were to tell you?"

"Who are they?"

"Harry and Larry."

"Okay, crazy lady, that's enough. I'd like you to leave."

"Just hear me out, please. I know this might sound a little weird, but I'm actually a psychic. I'm able to talk to ghosts."

"Of course you are. It's time for you to go now."

"I understand why you would be sceptical, but what do you have to lose? Is there anything I could do that could make you feel any worse than you already do?"

He shook his head.

"Okay. I'm going to need you to do something for me."

"What now?" he snapped.

"I want you to think of Harry and Larry. Close your

eyes so you can picture them."

"This is crazy."

"Please. Humour me."

He sighed, but shut his eyes anyway.

"Can you picture them?"

"It isn't difficult. I see their faces every day."

"Good. Now, I need you to invite them here."

"Do what?" He opened his eyes.

"Please. Just close your eyes, and invite them here."

"I invite you here," he said, with zero conviction.

"You don't have to say it out loud. You just need to think it, and more importantly, you have to mean it with all of your heart. Can you do that?"

"Okay, okay."

Nothing happened.

"You aren't trying hard enough. You have to believe. You have to mean it."

"Alright." His expression changed, and I could see the concentration etched on his face.

"That's it. Keep thinking those thoughts."

Just then, Harry and Larry appeared in the room. They both gave me a thumb's up.

"I've had enough of this." He opened his eyes, saw the two men, and took several steps backwards. "No! This can't be. I must be dreaming."

"This isn't a dream, Stewey," Harry said.

"It really is us." Larry smiled. "We have a lot to talk about."

"I think I'll leave you gentlemen to it." I started for the door.

Chapter 21

The next morning when I got to the office, Mrs V was singing. At least I think that's what the noise coming out of her mouth was.

What? Who are you calling cruel? You'd feel the same if you'd been forced to endure it.

"Good morning, Jill."

"You sound full of the joys of spring."

"Armi and I had such a wonderful evening at Ever."

"I take it the ballroom was a success?"

"It's fabulous. I'd expected recorded music, but your grandmother has a resident band down there."

"Is there enough room for one?"

"Plenty. It's strange. When we first got there, I didn't think the room would be big enough to accommodate everyone, but as the evening wore on, and more people arrived, the room seemed to get bigger." She laughed. "I know that must sound crazy."

Oh boy. That didn't sound crazy, but it did sound remarkably like magic to me.

"It looks like Grandma is onto another winner, then?"

"I reckon so. I heard lots of people say how much they'd enjoyed it, and that they intended to become regulars. When are you and Jack thinking of going?"

"As soon as I can talk him into it. There's something I wanted to ask you, Mrs V. I'm working on a case at the moment where I could do with your help."

"Ooh, how exciting! Do you want me to follow someone? I could wear a disguise."

"No, nothing like that. I need you to buy a garden gnome."

"A gnome?" She screwed up her face. "I hate those things."

"Me too, but I'm trying to catch a thief who's bringing loads of stolen goods into this world."

"World?"

"Did I say *world*? I meant country. They're bringing in lots of stolen goods, including gnomes. I need to catch them red-handed, and I thought you could pose as a potential gnome buyer."

"But what will my neighbours think?"

"You don't actually have to buy one. I just need you to get them to come around to your house. I'll do the rest."

"Alright, dear. If you think it will help."

I handed her the business card that Megan had given to me. "If you could ring this number, and arrange for them to call at your house, that would be great."

"Okay, Jill. I'll get straight on it."

Winky was no longer wearing his cowboy outfit. Instead, today, he was dressed as a fireman. If I'm being perfectly honest, I thought he made a better cowboy than a fireman, but who am I to judge?

"Is there any point in my asking why the outfit?"

"None."

"That's what I figured."

Once again, he had the camera set up on a tripod, and was taking photos of himself.

"Have you joined some kind of weird role-play dating site?"

"I don't ask questions about your private life, so keep your nose out of mine."

"Fair enough, but there's something else I want to talk

to you about."

"Hold on a minute." He took a few more photos, and then jumped up onto my desk. "Okay, what gives?"

"I've worked it out," I said.

"I don't have time for your cryptic clues." He sighed. "What is it you've worked out? How to be a P.I? Not before time."

"I know how you're able to offer the rental properties so cheaply on that Purrbnb app of yours."

"Really? Pray tell."

"You're getting cats to put properties on there when their owners are going away, aren't you?"

"How did you find out?"

"Seems like I'm a better P.I. than you give me credit for."

"Come on, tell me, how did you work it out?"

"Someone has moved into a house near to my sister. I'd seen it advertised on your app, but there's no way the old couple who live there would ever allow anyone to use it as a holiday home. Their cat must have done it. He knew when they were going on holiday. I'm right, aren't I?"

"So what if you are? No one gets hurt."

"Apart from the couple who own the house. It will be wrecked when they get home."

"No, it won't. The people renting it have to tidy it up or they'll get bad reviews, and never be able to use the service again."

"Who's going to give them a bad review? The owners know nothing about the arrangement."

"Not the owner. The person who listed the property."

"The cat?"

"Precisely. Now you see how it works."

"It just isn't right. I think you should pull the app, and close down the whole operation straightaway."

"Do you really feel that passionately about it?"

"Yes. I think it's outrageous."

"Let me think about it." He scratched his chin. "Okay, I've thought it through. No chance. If you think I'm giving up this goldmine just because it offends your sensibilities, then you're even more delusional than I thought you were."

***

Conrad Landers had been very convincing during our brief telephone conversation, but before I dismissed him entirely from my thinking, it occurred to me that I should talk to someone who had known him at the time of the murder. Back then, he and Patty Lake had both worked at the same garage, Meers Motors. My research had revealed that the garage had closed down seven years ago, but I was able to find an address for Colin Meers, the man who had owned it.

Rather than call ahead, I decided to go around to his house on spec.

The man tending the front garden was certainly in the right age group. His hair was grey, but quite thick for his age.

"Mr Meers?"

He looked up from his rose bed, and squinted at me. "Do I know you, young lady?"

"No. I wonder if I could talk to you about two of the people who used to work at your garage?"

"Sure. Do you mind if I carry on working while we

talk?"

"Not at all. You have a lovely garden."

"Thank you. It would be even better if it wasn't for the slugs. Who was it you wanted to talk about? As if I didn't know."

"Conrad Landers and Patty Lake."

"Are you the press?"

"No. I'm a private investigator. I'm working for Sophie Brownling. Her daughter, Angie, went missing around the same time as Patty was murdered."

"I remember. They never did find her, did they?"

"I'm afraid not. Can you tell me what kind of person Conrad was?"

"Not a murderer. That's for sure."

"You sound very sure about that?"

"I am. We worked together long enough for me to get to know him well. The only time I ever saw him lose his cool was when the rep from a tools company tried it on with Patty. She and Conrad were seeing each other at the time."

"What happened?"

"Nothing much. Conrad just gave him a bloody nose."

"What was Patty like?"

"Nice girl. Very pretty. She and Conrad weren't together for very long. I think she found someone else."

"How did Conrad take it?"

"He was upset, as you can imagine."

"Angry?"

"Maybe, but he would never have hurt Patty if that's what you're thinking."

"What about the bloodstained top that was found in Conrad's locker?"

"That's what did for him."
"Do you have any theories about how it got there?"
"No."
"But you still don't think Conrad did it?"
"I've never been surer of anything in my life. It's a crying shame what happened to that boy."

After leaving Colin Meers, I drove thirty miles to meet with Susan Bowles who was another one of the women who'd been with Angie Potts on the night of the disappearance.

She insisted on making tea, and plying me with cupcakes. The hardships I had to endure in this job.

"It only feels like yesterday," she said. "I can't believe it's twenty years ago."

"Do you think about it often?"

"All the time—even now. I can't begin to imagine what her mother must have gone through all these years. The not knowing must be unbearable."

"Do you remember much about that night?"

"If I'm honest, not really. To tell you the truth, I'd had way too much to drink. We all had, except for Angie."

"Oh? Wasn't she much of a drinker?"

"Angie?" Susan smiled. "She could really put it away, but not that night. She said she had a bad tummy."

"But she stayed until the end?"

"Yeah. We all went our separate ways at the same time. If I'd just waited with her, then maybe—" Her words trailed away.

"How do you mean?"

"Karen and Michelle got a taxi together. There was only one other taxi waiting. Angie insisted I take it. She said she'd wait for the next one. That was the last time I saw her." Susan choked on the words, and began to cry.

"Are you okay?"

"Yeah. I'm sorry. It still hurts even after all this time."

"Apart from the tummy bug, did Angie seem okay that night, do you remember?"

"She was her usual miserable self. I loved Angie to bits, but she was never the life and soul of the party. Not like she used to be when we were younger."

"Are you saying she'd changed?"

"Yeah. It hit her hard when her father died. She was never really the same person after that."

"How did she get on with her stepfather?"

"She didn't. She hated him."

"Why?"

"I don't know the ins and outs because she would never talk about him. She was never going to like the person who tried to take the place of her real dad."

"Do you have any theories about what might have happened to her that night?"

"I think some nutter must have picked her up in a car. Maybe someone posing as a taxi driver, but, I'm only guessing. Do you really think that you'll be able to get to the bottom of this, after all this time?"

"I don't know, but I'm going to give it my best shot."

***

The other person who'd been on the night out with Angie was Michelle Wright. I'd arranged to see her later that day, but for now, I had something else I needed to attend to.

I made a call.

"Lolly? It's Jill. I have some information about your boyfriend."

"What's he been up to?"

"You have nothing to worry about anymore."

"Oh? Why?"

"I've just seen him leave on a train."

"Where's he going?"

"Edinburgh. He had two suitcases with him, so I assume he's gone for good."

"To Edinburgh? Are you sure?"

"Positive. That's good news, isn't it?"

"Err—yeah—look, Jill, I have to go."

"What about my bill, Lolly?"

"I'll pop in later this week to pay it. Is that okay?"

"Sure. I look forward to seeing you then."

When I got back to the office, Winky was wearing a musketeer's outfit, complete with sword.

"Very dashing."

"Thank you. You're looking remarkably pleased with yourself."

"I am, and I have your gang to thank for it. I do believe I may have seen the last of Lolly Jolly. For some time, at least."

"What have you done with her? You haven't got her tied up in a basement somewhere, have you?"

"I should have thought of that. No, I've just sent her on a wild goose chase to Edinburgh."

"Nice one." Winky posed with his sword held aloft, and snapped a few photos.

"Are you going to tell me what's going on with all these

costumes?"
"No."

Mrs V came through to my office. "Why have you got him dressed up like that?" She was staring at Winky.
"I think it suits him, don't you?"
"He could do himself an injury with that sword. Not that I care. Anyway, I've just heard back from the gnome man. He's coming to my house tonight."
"That's great. He's in for a big surprise."

Chapter 22

I'd promised to go to Cuppy C to see the grand unveiling of the fish tank. To be perfectly honest, I wasn't overly keen to go. Seen one fish; seen too many fish. Aunt Lucy had been roped in too, so I'd said I'd meet her at her house, and we could walk over together.

I magicked myself over to Candlefield, and landed outside Aunt Lucy's front door. There was a removal van parked outside the neighbour's house.

"Hi!" A tall, young wizard, dressed in jeans and a polo shirt walked over to me. "I'm Glen. We're moving in next door."

"Nice to meet you. I'm Jill. This is my aunt's house."

"I met your aunt the other day. She seems very nice."

"She is. Are you by yourself today?"

"Yeah. My other half has to work, so she's left me to it. By the time she gets here, it should all be done."

"It sounds like she's got her head screwed on."

"Where do you want these?" One of the removal men shouted.

"I'd better go," Glen said. "I'm supposed to be supervising. Nice to meet you, Jill."

"You too."

Aunt Lucy was putting the finishing touches to her makeup.

"I've just seen your new neighbour."

"Glen? Nice young man, isn't he?"

"Seems like it."

"Who's a nice young man?" Grandma appeared out of nowhere.

"My new neighbour, mother."

"Neighbours? More trouble than they're worth. Are you going to make me a cup of tea or what? A person could die of thirst."

"I don't have time. Jill and I are going to see the unveiling of the twins' fish tank. Would you like to come with us?"

"No, I would not. The only fish I'm interested in are those next to my chips and mushy peas. Don't you have time to make me a cuppa before you go?"

"No, I don't, mother. You know where the kettle is."

"Charming. And here I am, exhausted from my new successful business venture."

"Mrs V said the ballroom was a resounding success," I said.

"Of course it was. What did you expect? I'll need to employ more staff."

Why don't you stop playing at detective, and come and run my ballroom?"

"Tempting an offer as that is, I'm going to have to decline. I do know someone who is looking for a job, though."

"Who's that?"

"Her name is Maria. She's just moved to Washbridge, and is going out with Luther, my accountant."

"Is she a human?"

"No. She's a sup. A vampire, actually."

"Vampire? They're an untrustworthy lot."

"That's something of a generalisation, isn't it? Maria seems sound enough to me."

"Does that mean you're vouching for her?"

"Err—I—err—I guess so."

"In that case, tell her to come and see me. If it doesn't work out, I'll know who to blame."

"Okay. While I've got you here, there's something I need to tell you about Yarnstormers, and I don't think you're going to like it."

"Hurry up then. Places to go, people to see."

"Ma Chivers owns it."

"And?"

"Didn't you hear what I said? Ma Chivers owns Yarnstormers."

"So?"

"I—err—thought you'd be—err—"

"*You* may have time to stand around here talking gibberish all day, but *I* don't. And it doesn't look like anyone is going to make me a cup of tea, so I may as well be on my way. Goodbye."

And with that, she was gone. I'd expected Grandma to explode when she found out about Ma Chivers, but she seemingly couldn't have cared less. That woman was an enigma wrapped up in a thingamabob.

Aunt Lucy and I set off for Cuppy C.

"Have you actually seen the tank the twins have bought?" Aunt Lucy said.

"Yeah. I was with them when they ordered it. It's massive. I tried to persuade them to go for something smaller, but you know what they're like."

"I certainly do."

"Are they expecting a big crowd?"

"I wouldn't have thought so. People are hardly going to be queuing around the block just to see a few fish, are they?"

"Did you hear what happened with the Tammy Winestock fiasco, Aunt Lucy?"

"I did, and I could kick myself for not getting there earlier that day. I could really use a book on asparagus."

And believe it or not, she said that with a straight face.

Aunt Lucy checked her watch. "We're running late. The twins won't be happy."

"We can blame Grandma. She slowed us down."

"If you've come to see the fish, I wouldn't bother." A grumpy, old wizard pushed past us as we walked into the shop.

"Total waste of time." A vampire was also headed for the door.

"What's going on?" Aunt Lucy said.

That's what I wanted to know too. From where I was standing, I could just about see the twins over the crowd. What I couldn't see was the giant fish tank.

It took me a few minutes, but I managed to push my way to the front; Aunt Lucy followed in my wake.

"Oh dear." I laughed.

The twins glared at me.

"Where's the fish tank?" Aunt Lucy said, then she spotted it, and she laughed too.

"Charming!" Pearl was red in the face. "I might have known you two would think this is funny."

"Sorry, girls." Aunt Lucy was trying, without much success, to stop laughing.

"That's smaller than I remember it." I pointed to the tiny fish bowl on the table, which had two goldfish in it.

"You're not funny, Jill." Amber scowled.

"What happened to the big tank? Don't tell me it

broke?"

"It's around the back in the alley," Pearl said.

"What's it doing out there?"

Pearl mumbled something under her breath.

"Sorry? What did you say?"

"I said, it won't fit through the door."

How I kept the laughter at bay, I'll never know. "I thought you had all the necessary dimensions?"

"She was the one who measured it." Amber pointed an accusatory finger at her sister. "But she failed to say she'd measured it in centimetres."

"I told you the measurements were in centimetres!" Pearl said.

"No, you didn't. You said they were in inches."

"I never mentioned inches."

"What are you going to do with the tank?" Aunt Lucy asked.

I got in quick before the twins could respond. "You could always fill it with water, and advertise it as an open-air swimming pool."

I managed to duck the first cupcake, but the second one caught me on the shoulder.

"Hey, stop! You're wasting good food."

The third one caught me smack bang on the chin.

***

To visit Michelle Wright by car would have meant a four-hour round trip, and I really couldn't face all that driving, so I magicked myself there.

What? I know I've said I don't like to use magic to move around the human world, but what can I tell you?

Sometimes I'm a rebel.

Michelle had told me on the phone that she was married, and had a daughter who'd just started at university.

"Have you already spoken to Karen and Susan?" she asked, once we were seated in the living room.

"Yes. They both gave me the impression that that night still weighs heavy on their minds, even after all this time."

"Really? Personally, I can't see the point in dragging all this up again. It can only cause pain to Angie's mother."

"She was the one who asked me to take another look at the disappearance."

"Even so. It can't be good for her."

"How would you feel if your daughter went missing? Do you think you'd be able to put it behind you? Ever?"

"I suppose not. Sorry."

"That's okay. I just have a few questions."

"Sure."

"How would you describe Angie?"

"How do you mean?"

"Was she a happy person?"

"She was happy enough. The same as the rest of us."

"Susan suggested that Angie was more subdued than the rest of the group. She said Angie changed after her father died?"

"I wouldn't have described her as subdued, but then I hadn't known her as long as Susan."

"What about her stepfather?"

"What about him?"

"Did Angie ever mention him?"

"Not that I remember."

"Susan suggested she didn't like him."

"I don't recall her ever saying that."

"How was Angie on the night she disappeared?"

"She was fine."

"Not poorly?"

"No."

"Was she drunk?"

"No more than the rest of us."

"What do you think happened to her?"

"I've no idea, and to be honest, I'd prefer not to think about it. I moved on with my life a long time ago, and in my opinion, it would be better if the others did the same. You can't seriously believe there is any realistic chance of finding Angie alive after so long?"

"I hope to find out what happened to her if only to give her mother closure."

"You're wasting your time, if you ask me."

Call it P.I. intuition if you like, but something about Michelle Wright just didn't ring true. Several of her answers contradicted those given by Susan and Karen. And whereas the other two women still seemed haunted by that night, Michelle seemed overly keen to forget it. I came away with the distinct impression that she was hoping to persuade me to drop the case. Why would she want that?

After leaving her apartment, and purely on a hunch, I cast the 'listen' spell. Sure enough, moments later, I heard Michelle make a phone call.

"It's me. Yes, she's just left. I don't know. I tried to tell her she was wasting her time, but she's very pushy. Your mum, yes. No, of course I didn't tell her anything. Yes, okay. I'll let you

know if I hear from her again. Okay, bye."

Hmm? It seemed my hunch had been right. Unless I was very much mistaken, Michelle Wright had just been speaking to Angie Potts. If that was true, one thing was obvious, Angie did not want to be found by her mother. That was of course her prerogative, but I had to at least speak to her, so I could find out why.

Michelle was quite obviously not expecting to see me again so soon.
"What do you want now?"
"Sorry. I got to the car and realised I hadn't got my car keys. I think I must have dropped them on your armchair."
"Oh? Okay, you'd better come through."
As soon as we were inside, and she'd closed the door, I cast the 'freeze' spell. I then grabbed her phone from the coffee table, and searched for the last number dialled. After making a note of it, I returned the phone, reversed the 'freeze' spell, and then cast the 'forget' spell on my way out of the door.
After magicking myself back to Washbridge, I found a quiet spot, and then called the number I'd taken from Michelle Wright's phone.
"Hello?"
"Angie? Angie Potts?"
"You've got the wrong number."
"Angie, don't hang up. I know it's you."
"I don't know what you're talking about."
"I've already traced your location," I lied. "I know you don't want your parents to know where you are, and I

promise I won't tell them, but only if you agree to meet with me."

"How do I know you're telling the truth? How do I know they won't turn up too?"

"You don't, I'm afraid. You'll just have to trust me."

"Okay. When? Where?"

"You name the time and place, and I'll be there."

***

I'd sent Jack a message to let him know I'd be late in. I told him that I was going to Mrs V's house for dinner. That wasn't entirely true. I was actually going there to try to catch the garden gnome thief, but I figured Jack didn't need to know that. He already thought I was crazy.

In the meantime, I went back to the office; there were paperclips that needed sorting.

Winky, who was still dressed as a musketeer, was jumping up and down, screaming at his phone. Something was obviously amiss.

"What's wrong?"

"It's a disaster!"

"What is?"

"The dates on the app somehow all got messed up. People are turning up for holiday rentals on the wrong week."

"How did that happen?"

"If I knew that, I'd sort it out. I've got dozens of cats ringing to tell me that guests have arrived one week early."

Just then, his phone rang.

"I know. Yes, the dates are wrong. I don't know. I'm

trying to sort it out."
 And I thought I had problems.
 Snigger.

Chapter 23

Before going to Mrs V's house, I wanted to grab a quick word with Luther.

"Jill?"

"Hi, Luther. I'm just calling to tell you that I may have found a job for Maria. Is she still looking for one? I don't have her number, or I'd have called her myself."

"I'm just with a client at the moment."

"Oh? Sorry. I—"

"That's okay. Why don't I give you her number so you can tell her yourself? I know she's still looking for something."

Maria picked up on the first ring.

"Maria, it's Jill. Luther gave me your number. Are you still looking for a job?"

"Yes, but I'm not having much joy. I have good references, but they're all from businesses in Candlefield. I can hardly use any of those over here."

"I've heard of a job that you might be interested in. It's a little unusual though."

"Right now, I'm prepared to consider anything."

"My grandmother has a shop on the high street. It's called Ever A Wool Moment. Have you seen it?"

"I don't think so."

"As the name suggests, it sells yarn and that kind of stuff, but it also has a tea room, a roof terrace, and she's just opened a ballroom in the basement."

"Wow! It sounds like there's a lot going on there."

"No kidding. Grandma likes to describe it as a *destination*. My sister, Kathy, already works there."

"How does she like it?"

"I'm not going to lie to you. She isn't in love with the place, but that's mainly because of Grandma. She can be—err—challenging."

"What exactly do you mean by *challenging*?"

"To be honest, she can be a real pain in the backside. She'll expect you to work harder than you've ever done in your life, and then spend all day criticising you."

"You're really selling this."

"I just want you to know what you'd be letting yourself in for. You would at least have the advantage of being a sup. Poor Kathy and Chloe are both humans, and have no idea what's going on, half the time."

"I really could do with a job."

"Why don't you think about it, and let me know?"

"No need. I'd like to go for it. Do you think your grandmother will consider my application?"

"I've already mentioned you to her, and she's prepared to give you a trial."

"Without even an interview?"

"Apparently, but I should warn you that she thinks all vampires are untrustworthy."

"Oh great."

"I shouldn't read too much into that. Grandma doesn't trust anyone. You'll see what I mean after you've been working there for a while. So, are you sure? Should I let her know that you want the job?"

"Yes, please."

"Okay. I'll get back to you with a start date."

"Great. Thanks, Jill."

Grandma took forever to pick up, and when she did

eventually answer, it was short and to the point.

"What do you want?"

"Charming."

"I'm busy with my bunions. Why are you disturbing me?"

"I've just been talking to Maria."

"Who?"

"The vampire I mentioned to you."

"Untrustworthy, the lot of them."

"She'd like to take the job. When do you want her to start?"

"Tomorrow at eight."

"Tomorrow? But—"

She'd ended the call.

"Maria?"

"Jill? That was quick."

"Grandma would like you to start tomorrow at eight. Is that okay?"

"Tomorrow? Sure, I guess so."

"Good luck, then."

She was sure going to need it.

***

I was beginning to have second thoughts about dragging Mrs V into this. Although not short of enthusiasm, she was clearly very nervous.

"Talk me through it one more time, Jill, would you?"

We were in the lounge of Mrs V's house, and had gone through the plan at least a dozen times.

"When he comes to the door, invite him in. He'll want

to make a quick sale, but I need you to keep him talking long enough so that I can get into his car."

"How will you do that if it's locked?"

"Don't worry about that. I have my methods."

"Won't it be dangerous? What if he sees you?"

"He won't. Stop worrying about me, and focus on what you're going to say to him."

"I could ask to see his catalogue."

"We've already talked about that. He won't have a catalogue, but he may have photos of the gnomes that he's trying to sell. You need to take your time looking through them. Make out that it's a difficult decision, and when he's been in the house for at least five minutes, tell him you'll need to talk to your husband when he gets home, and that you'll get back to him later."

"I don't have a husband."

Oh boy! "I know that, Mrs V. It's just what you need to say to get him out of the house."

"Of course. Sorry, Jill, I'm just a little nervous."

"Try to calm down. If you look nervous when he comes, he might smell a rat and do a runner.

"Why don't I make us both a cup of tea? That will settle my nerves."

"Good idea."

"I have a new packet of custard creams, if you'd like one?"

One?

Thirty minutes and four custard creams later, we were ready to rock and roll. Mrs V was in the lounge, practising her lines. I'd left the house through the back door, cast the 'invisible' spell, and was now standing on the drive, waiting for our target to arrive.

I didn't have long to wait. Tony Tallhats may have been a lying, thieving conman, but at least he was a punctual, lying, thieving conman.

He was ugly too. In fact, he gave ugly a bad name. Just as I'd suspected, he was a wizard. He'd obviously teamed up with a ghost, in order to fence goods that had been stolen from GT. As soon as the car pulled up in front of the house, I hurried down the drive. The plan was to duck inside the car before he had the chance to close the door. For once, good luck was on my side. After he'd stepped out of the car, he spent a few seconds straightening his creased jacket before pushing the door shut. That gave me more than enough time to sneak inside, and clamber into the back seat. All I had to do now was wait, and hope that Mrs V didn't lose her nerve, and give the game away.

After ten minutes, I was beginning to worry. If he'd realised that Mrs V was trying something on, and he'd hurt her in any way, I'd never forgive myself. I should never have put her in that situation. What was I thinking?

I was just about to force my way out of the car when Mrs V's front door opened, and Ugly stepped out. Even though I couldn't hear what was being said, it was obvious that he was still trying to close the sale, but Mrs V was having none of it. In the end, he nodded, smiled and then walked away.

Well done, Mrs V!

The car journey was painful because Ugly insisted on singing along to the radio. The man was tone deaf, and didn't know half of the lyrics; he just made them up as he went along. It came as something of a relief when he pulled up outside a large, lock-up garage.

Fortunately, Ugly didn't bother to lock the car door behind him, so I waited until he was in the garage, and then followed. The small window on the side of the building was ajar. The gap wasn't wide enough for anyone to get through, unless of course they were really tiny. Cue the 'shrink' spell. Mini-me levitated my way through the window. Once inside, I was hidden from view behind a pile of ornamental plant pots. Even though I couldn't see Ugly, I could hear him talking to someone.

"Where are the rest?" Ugly demanded.

"This is all I could get."

"I've only got three gnomes left. What do I do then? I've just been speaking to an old gal who's going to call me later. She's going to take one—maybe two. Then what am I supposed to do? I've got ads in all the local shops."

"Don't worry. I've found a great new source. There are dozens of them."

"So where are they?"

"Keep your wig on. I got hold of two, but then a police car came down the road so I had to store them in the garden of the house across the road. I should be able to get them tonight, and a load more too, probably."

"You'd better. I could do with some more garden chairs, too."

"No worries. I'm on it."

Although I couldn't see Ugly's partner in crime, I knew he must be the ghost who was stealing garden furniture and tools, and bringing them through to the human world. From what I'd just heard, it sounded as though he'd earmarked Alberto's garden as a prime source for garden gnomes. That gave me pause for thought. Maybe

I'd be doing Mum a favour if I let this guy go, so he could clear their garden of all those stupid gnomes. No! That would be allowing my gnomist views to influence my decisions.

I'd heard enough; it was time for action.

Or at least it would have been if I'd had the good sense to get clear of the plant pots before reversing the 'shrink' spell. Instead, I tripped, and fell headfirst into a pile of deck chairs.

"Who's that?" Ugly shouted.

"Hi." I treated him to my best smile, as I disentangled myself from the deck chairs and plant pots.

"How did you get in here?"

"I'm not sure that matters." Back on my feet, I dusted myself down. "What's important, is that you two are busted."

"Two?" The ghost, who was clearly wearing a toupee, sounded shocked. "You can't see me."

"Yeah. That's where you're wrong." Before either of them had the chance to react, I cast the 'tie-up' spell, and bound them hand and foot.

"Let me go!" Ugly shouted. "This is all a mistake. I didn't know these goods were stolen."

"You can tell that to the rogue retrievers."

"What about me?" the ghost said.

"Something tells me you'll both be going away for a long time."

Back outside the garage, I made two calls. The first to Daze; the second to Constance.

Mission accomplished. Alberto's gnomes were safe.

More's the pity.

***

Angie Potts had only agreed to meet me because she was afraid I would let her mother know where she was now living. She'd insisted on meeting in a hotel on the outskirts of Chester.

This time, I'd resisted the urge to use magic to travel, but after being stuck in traffic for almost an hour, I was beginning to regret my decision. By the time I got to the hotel, I wasn't sure if Angie would still be waiting, or if she would have lost patience and left.

There were only three people in the lounge bar: Two men seated at the bar, and a woman, by herself, at the far side of the room.

"Angie?"

"I didn't think you were coming. I was just about to leave."

"Sorry. I got caught in traffic. Can I get you another drink?"

"Yes, please. I'll take another rum and coke."

I ordered her drink, and a soda water for myself.

"Thanks." She took a long drink. "I wish you hadn't found me."

"How have you managed to stay out of sight for all these years?"

"It was difficult at first, but it got easier. I have a new identity and a new life now. I don't want to ruin that."

"Do you have a family here?"

"No. I never married. I was engaged once, but it didn't work out."

"Your mother hired me to look into your disappearance. She assumes you're dead, but she still needs closure."

"You haven't told her that you've found me, have you?"

"No. I promised I wouldn't. Why don't you want her to know? You must realise what she's been going through all this time. She loves you."

"Too little, too late." Angie's tone had changed; there was a much harder edge to it now. "She didn't care when it mattered."

"What do you mean?"

"Have you met *him*?"

"Him? Are you talking about your stepfather?"

"He was no father; he was a monster."

"What did he do?"

"He hated me from the first time he met me. I was just an obstacle between him and Mum. He wanted me gone; he told me as much."

"What did he do? Was he violent towards you?"

"Sometimes, but it was mainly psychological rather than physical abuse. Whenever we were alone, he would tell me how useless I was. How I'd never amount to anything, and how no one would ever want me. Sometimes, he'd lash out and hit me, but he was careful never to leave any bruises."

"Why didn't you tell your mum?"

"I did. She didn't believe me. All she could see was her perfect new husband. She accused me of making it up just to get rid of him."

"Is that why you decided to disappear?"

"It wasn't only that."

"What then?"

"I saw him with another woman in a bar—they were kissing."

"What did you do?"

"I told him that I'd seen him, and threatened to tell Mum. He told me if I said anything he'd kill me. The way he said it, I believed him. That's when I started planning my escape."

"Why didn't you tell your mother that you were leaving?"

"I don't know. I suppose I wanted to punish her because she'd let me down."

"Do you know who the woman with your stepfather was?"

"I don't know her name, but I followed her. She worked at a garage."

"Do you happen to remember the name of that garage?"

Angie shook her head.

"Could it have been Meers Motors?"

"That was it. My stepfather sold tools for a living; he probably chatted her up when he was visiting the garage on business."

I took out my phone, and did a quick Google search to find the image I needed.

"Was this the woman who was with your father that day?"

"I think so. It looks like her. How did you know?"

"This is Patty Lake. She was murdered a few months after you disappeared."

Angie continued to stare at the photo, and didn't speak for several minutes.

"Are you okay?" I said.

"She was murdered?"

"You must have known?"

"I had no idea. After I left, I never looked back. I had no reason to keep up with the news in Washbridge."

"Surely, Michelle mentioned it at the time?"

"Back then, Michelle didn't know I'd deliberately disappeared any more than the others did. I bumped into her in Liverpool about six years ago; she thought she'd seen a ghost. I made her promise never to tell anyone that she'd seen me, and she's kept her word. We've stayed in touch ever since then. Did they get anyone for the murder?"

"They convicted a man named Conrad Landers. He's been in prison for almost twenty years, and has always proclaimed his innocence. You and I now know that he's probably telling the truth."

"You think my stepfather murdered her?"

"It's possible—probable even. And I want you to help me to prove it."

I'd just arrived back home from Chester when my phone rang; it was Aunt Lucy.

"Jill! It's terrible." She sounded distraught.

"What's wrong?"

"The new neighbour."

"Glen? What's he done?"

"Not Glen. It's his partner. I've just seen her. It's Alicia."

"What?"

"She came over and introduced herself—all nice as pie."

"She's got some front, that one."

"She apologised for her behaviour in the past, and said it's all behind her now. She reckons that since she met Glen, she's distanced herself from Ma Chivers."

"Do you believe her?"

"I don't know what to think."

"I do. A leopard never changes its spots. We'll have to

keep an eye on her. Will you be okay?"

"Yes, I'm fine. It was just such a shock."

"Okay, well you know where I am if you need me."

Alicia, a changed woman? I'd believe that when I saw it. No, come to think of it, I wouldn't even believe it then.

Chapter 24

The next morning, I didn't bother going into the office. Instead, after parking my car in Washbridge city centre, I magicked myself over to the airship departure point in Candlefield.

The man behind the turnstile checked my ticket, stamped it, and handed it back to me. The waiting room was deserted, which was hardly surprising given that it was a school holiday at CASS. On my previous visit, I'd been accompanied by the caretaker, Reggie, but it looked as though I'd be travelling alone this time.

I didn't have long to wait until the airship arrived, and on this trip, I was able to relax and take in all of the scenery. Just as on my previous visit, we landed on the playing fields where Desdemona Nightowl was waiting to greet me.

"Jill. Good to see you again."

"It's good to be back."

"I'm glad I was able to greet you in person this time. Hopefully, this visit won't be marred by any unwanted intruders."

"Fingers crossed."

During my previous visit, the walls had been breached by a pouchfeeder who had grabbed one of the pupils. It was while helping to rescue the young boy that I'd discovered the secret passage in which the portrait had later been found.

"I know that you're particularly keen to find out more about the history of CASS," Ms Nightowl said.

"That's right. I'm also hoping to find out more about the portrait that you gave me."

"I've arranged for you to spend some time with Doreen Littletoes. She teaches history here at CASS, but she also has a personal interest in the history of the school, the building, and the Wrongacre family. If anyone can help you, Doreen can."

I was quite relieved when Ms Nightowl led the way back to the main building on foot; I hadn't been looking forward to another hair-raising trip aboard the mini hovercraft. We entered the building via the front entrance. It was the first time I'd seen that part of the school; it was truly breathtaking. The huge wooden double-doors opened onto an enormous reception hall. A double staircase wound up to the balconied floor above.
"This is amazing."
"I'm sorry you didn't get to see any of this on your last visit. This part of the building is almost exactly the same as it was when the Wrongacre family lived here."
"It must cost a small fortune to maintain."
"It most certainly does."
The sound of footsteps on the wooden stairs caught our attention.
"Ah, here's Doreen now."
Littletoes by name, but not by nature. Doreen was a diminutive woman, bent almost double with age. Everything about her was small and fragile. Everything that is apart from her feet, which were enormous. The sound of her boots on the wooden stairs echoed all around the large hall.
"Doreen, may I introduce Jill Gooder?"
"I'm so very pleased to meet you, Ms Gidder."
"Gooder." Ms Nightowl corrected her.

"Sorry. I had been hoping to meet you on your last visit, Ms Gidder, but then the awful pouchfeeder put paid to that."

"Very nice to meet you, too, Miss Littletoes."

"Please call me Doreen."

"And you must call me Jill."

"Lill it is."

"Can I leave *Jill* with you, Doreen?" Ms Nightowl said.

"Of course, headmistress."

"Right, I'll catch up with you later, Jill." Ms Nightowl disappeared down one of the many corridors which led off the main hall.

"I thought we could work out of my office, Lill."

"Err—it's Jill, actually. Yes, that would be great."

"This way then, Lill."

Doreen clomped her way back up the staircase, with me in tow.

"My office is in the East Wing. I hope you don't mind the walk. I don't like those horrible hover thingies. They give me a migraine."

"No problem. It will give me a chance to see more of the school."

And there was a lot to see. Beautiful works of art: paintings, sculptures, and tapestries lined all of the corridors.

"Isn't it dangerous to have these pieces on display? With so many children rushing back and forth, surely things must get damaged?"

"The children aren't allowed in this part of the building unless they are accompanied by a member of staff. There are many different ways to navigate the school. The children have their own staircases and corridors. Those are kept free of anything which might be damaged. This whole building is something of a maze. I've worked here for longer than I care to remember, and I still get lost from time to time."

We'd been walking for at least ten minutes when I noticed a tapestry that looked familiar. I'd seen an identical one a couple of minutes earlier. I wasn't sure whether there were two of them, or if we'd simply been walking around in circles. I was trying to think of a polite way to ask if we were lost when Doreen came to a halt in front of a door.

"Here we are. I hope you'll excuse the mess, Lill. I haven't had the chance to tidy up today."

"No problem." I followed her inside.

The room probably did have walls, but they weren't visible because of the huge piles of books which hemmed us in on all sides. The room was illuminated by a small chandelier. If there was a window in there, that too was hidden behind the books.

"Do join me." Doreen sat on the green chaise longue which was the only surface not covered by books. "Ms Nightowl said that you're interested in the history of CASS. I could probably talk non-stop about that for a week. Was there anything in particular you'd like me to cover?"

"Primarily, I'm hoping to find out more about the woman who appears in the portrait that Ms Nightowl gave to me. It was found in a secret passageway here at CASS." I took out my phone, and brought up the photo I'd taken of the portrait.

Doreen put on the glasses that were hanging from a chain around her neck. "Oh yes, Ms Nightowl showed this to me."

"There's a similar portrait in this locket." I took it from around my neck, opened it, and held it out for her to see. "I think it's the same woman."

Doreen glanced back and forth between the photo and the locket. "I think you're right."

"I believe she may have some connection to this building. Do you have any idea who she might be?"

Doreen didn't respond; she seemed lost in her own thoughts.

"Doreen?"

"The woman? No, I don't know who she is." She pointed to the locket. "But, I may know who the man is."

"Really? Who?"

"I could be wrong. I probably am."

"Tell me. Please."

"This picture fits the description of Damon Wrongacre; the only son of Charles Wrongacre."

Some time ago, in Candlefield, I'd tried to research CASS and the Wrongacre family. I'd had limited success, and what little information I'd uncovered had been courtesy of a woman named Margaret Smallside. She'd mentioned Wrongacre's son, Damon.

"What makes you think this is Wrongacre's son? I understood that there were no portraits of him?"

"That's right. Charles had them all removed after his son's death, and no one has ever been able to find them since. I could very well be wrong, but I have seen a number of references to the son, and one thing that is always mentioned is his red hair and beard."

"Do you know much about him?"

"Practically nothing, other than that he died shortly

before he was due to marry."

"Marry who?"

"No one knows."

"It must have been the woman in the portrait. Why else would both of their pictures be in the locket?"

"That would make sense."

"There are initials on the locket." I turned it over so Doreen could see them.

"JB?"

"Does that mean anything to you?"

She shook her head. "Could those be the woman's initials?"

"I suppose that's possible, but that brings us back to square one. Who is the woman?"

Although we made no more progress on identifying the woman, I did find the time I spent with Doreen to be fascinating. Her knowledge of the building and CASS was exceptional. She could name every headmaster and headmistress who had ever led the school. She knew the story behind all of the house names. She'd even created a map that showed all the known secret passageways—I noted that 'mine' had recently been added.

The time flew by, and I was quite shocked to realise I'd been there for almost two hours.

"Do you think I might take a look around the building?" I said.

"Of course. The headmistress said that you were allowed to go wherever you wish. We're due to join her for lunch in an hour, so maybe we could look around until then?"

"Sounds good."

"I'm sorry, Lill, but my bladder isn't what it used to be. Would you mind waiting here while I go to the loo?"

"Of course not."

As I waited outside Doreen's office, I suddenly developed goose bumps on my arms. The temperature seemed to have dropped by several degrees, just as it did when I was visited by a ghost. But I could now see ghosts at will, and there were none around. And yet, I sensed some kind of presence. It was as though some inner sense was drawing me along the corridor. A similar thing had happened on my previous visit when I'd known instinctively where to find the hidden passageway.

I came upon a set of narrow stairs, and without hesitation, I hurried up them. They led to a much narrower corridor. Here, the walls were bare and in need of redecoration; the floor was bare wood. At the end of the short corridor was a door. Something told me that I had to get inside that room.

I tried the rusted handle, but the door wouldn't budge.

"Lill!" Doreen appeared at the top of the stairs; she was red in the face, and out of breath. "I thought I'd lost you."

"Sorry, Doreen. I should have waited for you."

"What are you doing up here?"

"I don't know. I was just wandering around and saw the stairs."

"There's nothing to see up here. This section of the building is no longer used."

"Do you know what's in this room?"

"Nothing, I would imagine."

"Is it possible to look inside?"

"Have you tried the door?"

"Yes, it's locked."

"I can try to find a key, if you really want to see inside?"

"Yes, please."

To my amazement, Doreen produced a small walkie-talkie from her bag. "Reggie? Come in. Are you there? Over."

"This is Reggie. Over." The familiar voice crackled through the speaker.

"Reggie. I'm with Lill Gidder. Over."

"Who? Over."

"Lill Gidder. Over."

"Oh, you mean Jill Gooder. Over."

"That's right. We're in the East Wing, in the upper corridor, on the floor above my office. Do you know where I mean? Over."

"I think so, but there's nothing up there, is there? Over."

"Lill would like to look in the room at the end of the corridor, but it's locked. Do you have a key? Over."

"I'm sure I do, somewhere. I'll be with you in a few minutes. Over."

"Okay. Over and out."

Less than five minutes later, Reggie came up the stairs.

"Hello again." He flashed me a smile. "How was your journey?"

"Quiet. I was the only passenger on the airship."

"It's ages since I was up here. Is there any particular reason why you want to see inside this room?"

"I just have a sense that there's something in there that I need to see. I can't explain it. It's the same feeling I had when I found the secret passageway the last time I was here."

"Okay. Let's take a look. It should be one of these keys."

He held out a huge key ring which held at least fifty keys. "Not that one. No. No. Not that one." He slowly worked his way through the keys. "That's it! That's the one!"

The key turned in the lock, and he pushed the door open. Doreen and I followed him inside.

The walls were bare, and there wasn't a single stick of furniture in the room. And yet, I still had the sense that I needed to be in there.

"Miss Gooder!" Desdemona Nightowl's voice echoed in the corridor. Moments later, she came through the door. "I have just received an urgent communication from Candlefield. You're needed back there immediately."

"Who is the communication from?"

"Your grandmother and the Combined Sup Council. They say it is a matter of life and death."

"Can I contact them?"

"I'm afraid not. There's no way to communicate directly with Candlefield from here. That's why your grandmother used the HurryBird to deliver the message."

If the message had come solely from Grandma, I might have ignored it. Her idea of life and death could easily have been something as trivial as her running out of bunion cream. But the fact that it had also been signed by the Combined Sup Council suggested that something serious had happened.

"How quickly can I get the airship back to Candlefield?"

"It's already waiting for you."

Chapter 25

When we were still some distance from Candlefield, the rain started to pound against the windows of the airship; the noise was deafening.

I was really nervous when we began our descent because visibility was terrible. Thankfully, the pilot knew his stuff, and we managed to land without incident. As soon as I stepped off the airship, I was greeted by Grandma, several of the Combined Sup Council, and a number of other level six witches.

"You took your time." Grandma stepped forward.

"I came as soon as I got your message. What's wrong?"

"Isn't it obvious?" She pointed at the window.

"I can't see anything because of the rain."

"The rain is the problem."

"Hold on. Are you telling me that you dragged me back here because it's raining?"

"This isn't normal rain. Candlefield has never seen rain as heavy as this. Two small rivers have already burst their banks, and the River Candle will do the same within a couple of hours. If that happens, a good part of Candlefield will be swept away."

"That's terrible, but I still don't know what you expect me to do about it."

"As I've already said, this isn't normal. The rain has been caused by magic."

"Are you talking about the 'rain' spell?"

"A variation of it, but this one is a thousand times more powerful."

"Can't you stop it?"

"Don't you think we've tried?" She pointed to the other

level six witches. "Even with our combined powers, we've been unable to overcome it. Whoever cast this spell has powers much greater than anything we've ever witnessed. That's why we called you back."

"What makes you think I can stop it?"

"If you can't, this could be the end of Candlefield. Why are we standing around here talking?"

Grandma led the way outside. Everyone had an umbrella; everyone except me. Within minutes, I looked like a drowned rat, but I didn't have time to worry about that. I had to stop the rain somehow.

All eyes were on me.

I knew how to cast the 'rain' spell, and I knew how to reverse it, but then so did all the other witches who were gathered around me. This was going to take every last ounce of my power.

I closed my eyes and focussed. Nothing happened; the rain continued to pour. I tried again, but still the rain came down. My energy levels were falling rapidly. I knew I could manage just one more attempt, but if that failed — I didn't even want to think about it.

I tried again.

I was so exhausted I could barely stand, but at least the rain had stopped. Everyone put down their umbrellas.

"Well done, Jill!"

"Bravo!"

The plaudits came thick and fast.

"Took you long enough, didn't it?" No prizes for guessing whose response that was.

"Who do you think cast the 'rain' spell, Grandma?"

"I have no idea, but whoever it was represents a real danger to Candlefield. This is the first threat I've ever encountered where a group of level six witches have been unable to combat it. That's a scary thought."

"Why would anyone do something like this? Why would they want to destroy Candlefield?"

"Perhaps they didn't."

"What do you mean? They almost did just that."

"That's true, but maybe that wasn't their primary aim."

"Sorry, you've lost me."

"Where were you when the rain started?"

"You know where I was. At CASS."

"And what were you doing there?"

"Just visiting."

"Are you sure that's all you were doing?"

"What does any of this have to do with the rain?"

"Perhaps someone didn't want you at CASS. Perhaps someone didn't want you doing whatever it was you were doing there. What better way to get you back here than to threaten Candlefield with destruction? Think about that, young lady. It seems to me that you may have a powerful enemy."

***

I magicked myself back to Washbridge.

As I made my way to the office, I thought about what Grandma had said, but I just didn't buy it. I was as concerned as she was about who was behind this, but the suggestion that it had all been to get me back from CASS was simply too far-fetched. It wasn't as though I'd found anything there anyway. My so-called instincts had led me on a wild goose chase to an empty room.

"What happened to you, Jill?" Jules gave me a horrified

look when I dripped my way into the room.

"I got caught in the rain."

She glanced out of the window. "It's been blue skies all morning."

"I was caught in a shower in Smallwash."

"It must have been a really heavy one."

"Look at the state of you!" Winky laughed. He was dressed as a pilot. "Been swimming?"

"Shut up, you! Haven't you got angry holiday customers to worry about?"

"Nah. That's all sorted."

"How?"

"I took down the app. It was more trouble than it was worth."

"What about all of the existing bookings? What are you going to do about the people whose holidays you've messed up?"

"I'll refund them, of course." He shrugged.

"You sound remarkably relaxed about all of this."

"Every successful entrepreneur must be prepared to fail, and be capable of bouncing back. That's just how it goes." He glanced down. "Don't you think you should towel yourself down? You're making puddles."

"I don't have a towel."

"I do."

"Great."

"The hire charge is five pounds."

"You're going to charge me to use a towel?"

"These are hard times. A cat has to make a living somehow."

I handed over the cash, and he produced a towel from

under the sofa.

"You could at least tell me what's going on with all these outfits you're wearing," I said, while towelling myself down.

"It's for my calendar."

"What calendar?"

"The one I'll be selling at the end of the year. How many should I put you down for?"

***

I'd just about dried off by the time Angie Potts arrived at the office.

"I'm still not sure about this, Jill." She looked as nervous as a kitten.

"We talked this through when I came to see you. You owe it to Patty Lake and Conrad Landers."

"But how can you be sure my stepfather murdered Patty?"

"You know what he's capable of—that he can be violent. Plus, you know he was seeing Patty."

"That doesn't mean he murdered her."

"If Conrad Landers is innocent, then someone planted Patty's top in his locker. In his job, your stepfather was a regular visitor to the garage. No one would have thought anything of it if they'd seen him there. He had ample opportunity to plant the evidence."

"But after all this time, what good can any of this do?"

"If my hunch is right, and your stepfather did murder Patty, then it's possible there are other victims, or that he could strike again. Would you want that on your conscience?"

"No, of course not, but I'm terrified of him."

"You have nothing to worry about. I'll be right there with you."

"What about my mother?"

"I've already thought of that. It will only complicate things if she's there when you turn up. I called her earlier and asked her to come and see me. In fact, she should be here in about thirty minutes. My PA has instructions to keep her occupied until we've done what we need to do."

"I'm still really worried about this."

"Come on." I grabbed her by the hand. "We have to go now."

Angie was silent during the drive to her mother's place. All the way there, I was half expecting her to demand to be let out of the car, but to my relief, her nerve held.

I parked two streets away from Sophie's bungalow.

"I never thought I'd be back here." She stared out of the window.

"You can do this. You have nothing to worry about; I'll be close by."

"Promise?"

"I promise. Off you go. Just knock on the door."

"Where will you be?"

"Nearby."

As soon as Angie was out of sight, I cast the 'invisible' spell, and followed her. When she reached the gate, she hesitated, and for a horrible moment, I thought she might turn tail, and run back to the car. Instead, she took a deep breath, and walked up to the door. I kept pace with her all the way.

It took her stepfather a few seconds to register what he

was seeing. That was hardly surprising as it was twenty years since he'd last seen Angie.

"What the hell are you doing here?" He looked up and down the street to see if anyone else was around.

"Either you talk to me, or I go to the police." The nerves were evident in her voice, but she'd remembered the line we'd rehearsed. I was so proud of her.

"Get inside." He grabbed her by the arm, and pulled her into the house. I managed to slip in behind her before he slammed the door closed.

"What's your game?" he demanded.

"I'm not scared of you anymore."

"You should be."

"Why? Because you murdered Patty?"

The colour drained from his face, and he took a step back. "What did you say?"

"You heard me. You killed her, and I'm going to tell the police everything I know."

"You stupid little cow! Do you think I'm going to let you ruin my life?"

"You can't stop me."

"I stopped Patty when she threatened to tell Sophie about our affair. I'll stop you too."

That was my cue to act. I quickly stepped into the lounge so that I would be out of sight when I reversed the 'invisible' spell.

"Don't lay a finger on her!" Visible now, I stepped back into the hallway.

"Where did you come from?" he yelled at me.

"That's not important. What matters is that I've just witnessed your confession, and I have it recorded on this." I showed him the digital recorder.

"Give me that!"

He tried to snatch it, but I'd already cast the 'power' spell, so I was able to overpower him easily. I told Angie to go outside and call the police. While she was doing that, I used the 'tie-up' spell on him.

***

It was one week later, and I'd arranged to meet Harry and Larry outside Coffee Triangle. They were both keen to see if there were any ideas they could 'steal' to use in Spooky Wooky.

When they appeared, I ushered them into the alleyway at the side of the shop.

"Don't forget. I'm the only one who can see you, so please don't go picking anything up or moving things."

"Don't worry." Harry grinned. "We're just here to observe and learn."

"Great. Okay then, let's go."

"Just a minute, Jill," Larry said. "We thought you should know that we had a long talk with Stewey after you left."

"How did that go?"

"He was really nervous at first, but once he got used to the idea of talking to a couple of ghosts, he came around. We managed to convince him that he has nothing to reproach himself for."

"That's great. Let's hope he'll be able to put his life back together now."

"I don't think there's any doubt about that. We managed to persuade him that he should open a brand-new bakery."

"You did? That's fantastic."

"Even better, we're going to help him do it. He seemed really keen for us to get involved."

It was tambourine day. Once I'd been served, I found a vacant table, while Harry and Larry took a look around the place.

I was barely half way through my muffin when Sophie and Angie walked through the door.

"Jill, your PA said we'd find you here," Sophie said. "I hope you don't mind."

"Not at all. Can I get you a drink?"

"Nothing for us, thanks. We just wanted a quick word."

They took seats opposite me.

"I take it that you two are reconciled."

"Angie has been kind enough to forgive me."

"There's nothing to forgive, Mum." Angie put her hand on her mother's.

"Of course there is. If I'd believed you when you told me about Lionel, twenty years ago, I would never have lost you. I'll never forgive myself for that. I've been living with that monster all of this time. I'm such a blind fool."

"Have they charged him with Patty's murder?" I asked.

"From what I hear, he's going to plead guilty to a charge of manslaughter."

"That's good news for Conrad Landers. I assume he'll be released soon."

"That poor man." Sophie shook her head. "Twenty years of his life wasted."

"Conrad made the ideal fall guy. Lionel and he had had an altercation some months before the murder. Lionel had come on to Patty while she was seeing Conrad. From all accounts, Conrad had given him a bloody nose. Planting Patty's top in Conrad's locker not only shifted suspicion from Lionel, it also gave him revenge for being humiliated by the younger man."

"It's just a pity it has taken so many years for justice to be finally done."

"True. Will you be moving back to Washbridge, Angie?"

"No. I've made a life for myself in Chester now. I have a good job and friends there. I intend to visit Mum regularly, though. And she can visit me whenever she likes."

"Thank you again, Jill," Sophie said. "You'll let me have your bill, I assume?"

"I will."

They stood up, and were about to leave when they both seemed to do a double-take. I followed their gaze, and realised that Larry had taken the seat next to me; he was shaking the tambourine. To Sophie and Angie, it appeared that the tambourine was shaking itself.

I snatched it from his hand.

"How? Err?" Sophie began to splutter.

I quickly cast the 'forget' spell, and then wished them goodbye.

"Sorry about that. I got carried away," Larry said, after they'd gone. Harry had now joined us at the table.

"You'll both have to be more careful if you're going to spend time in this world."

"Who are you talking to?" the young barista said. I hadn't spotted him walking over to my table.

"Me? Err—no one—I was just talking to myself."

"Right?" He looked mightily confused. "Are you Jill

Gooder?"

"That's me."

"I thought so. I have some good news for you."

"Oh?"

"You won the 'how many marbles in the jar' competition."

"I did? That's great. What did I win?"

"Stay there, and I'll go and get your prize."

I was so excited. Just wait until I told Jack that I'd won.

Oh no!

"It's rather big. Do you think you'll be able to manage it?" He was holding one of the giant triangles they'd used in the recent promotion.

I pushed past him, and sprinted for the door.

"Hey! Wait! You've forgotten your prize!"

ALSO BY ADELE ABBOTT

The Witch P.I. Mysteries:

Witch Is When... (Books #1 to #12)
Witch Is When It All Began
Witch Is When Life Got Complicated
Witch Is When Everything Went Crazy
Witch Is When Things Fell Apart
Witch Is When The Bubble Burst
Witch Is When The Penny Dropped
Witch Is When The Floodgates Opened
Witch Is When The Hammer Fell
Witch Is When My Heart Broke
Witch Is When I Said Goodbye
Witch Is When Stuff Got Serious
Witch Is When All Was Revealed

Witch Is Why... (Books #13 to #24)
Witch Is Why Time Stood Still
Witch is Why The Laughter Stopped
Witch is Why Another Door Opened
Witch is Why Two Became One
Witch is Why The Moon Disappeared
Witch is Why The Wolf Howled
Witch is Why The Music Stopped
Witch is Why A Pin Dropped
Witch is Why The Owl Returned
Witch is Why The Search Began
Witch is Why Promises Were Broken
Witch is Why It Was Over

Witch Is How... (Books #25 to #36)
Witch is How Things Had Changed
Witch is How Poison Tasted Good
Witch is How The Mirror Lied
Witch is How The Tables Turned
Witch is How The Drought Ended
Witch is How The Dice Fell
Witch is How The Biscuits Disappeared
Witch is How Dreams Became Reality
Witch is How Bells Were Saved
Witch is How To Fool Cats
Witch is How To Lose Big
Witch is How Life Changed Forever

The Susan Hall Mysteries:
Whoops! Our New Flatmate Is A Human.
Whoops! All The Money Went Missing.

AUTHOR'S WEB SITE
http:www.AdeleAbbott.com

FACEBOOK
http://www.facebook.com/AdeleAbbottAuthor

MAILING LIST
(new release notifications only)
http:/AdeleAbbott.com/adele/new-releases/

Printed in Great Britain
by Amazon